I LOST MY GRANNY IN THE SUPERMARKET

JO SIMMONS

Illustrated by NATHAN REED

BLOOMSBURY
CHILDREN'S BOOKS

LONDON   OXFORD   NEW YORK   NEW DELHI   SYDNEY

BLOOMSBURY CHILDREN'S BOOKS
Bloomsbury Publishing Plc
50 Bedford Square, London WC1B 3DP, UK
29 Earlsfort Terrace, Dublin 2, Ireland

BLOOMSBURY, BLOOMSBURY CHILDREN'S BOOKS
and the Diana logo are trademarks of Bloomsbury Publishing Plc

First published in Great Britain in 2021 by Bloomsbury Publishing Plc

A catalogue record for this book is available from the British Library

ISBN: PB: 978-1-5266-2046-0; eBook: 978-1-5266-2045-3

2 4 6 8 10 9 7 5 3 1

Printed and bound in Great Britain by CPI Group (UK) Ltd,
Croydon CR0 4YY

To find out more about our authors and books visit www.bloomsbury.com
and sign up for our newsletters

For Lyn, the grooviest granny of all

CHAPTER ONE

'Mum!' Harry shouted. 'Primrose and Daisy are in the garden.'

Harry spotted them from his seat at the kitchen table, where he was eating breakfast. Primrose and Daisy were next door's goats.

Only they weren't next door any more. They had broken into Harry's garden and were devouring his mum's flowers.

From upstairs, Harry heard a screech from his mum.

'Get ready,' he said to Kerry, his teenage sister, who was sitting opposite.

Mum raced into the kitchen, grabbed a saucepan and a wooden spoon and, banging the two together, steamed out into the garden, her skirt billowing around her. Harry imagined her as some sort of rubbish superhero. Pan Woman—Goat Nemesis!

Harry and Kerry carried on spooning cereal into their mouths, while their mum raced after the goats, shouting, 'Get out of it, you filthy animals!'

'She shouldn't talk to them like that,' Harry muttered. 'Goats have feelings too.'

Eventually, after Primrose had butted Mum and Daisy had eaten a tea towel off the washing line, Mum managed to herd the animals back into the neighbouring garden.

'This is going to be my fault, isn't it? I can tell by the way she's walking. That's the "I need to speak to Harry about this" walk,' Harry said, as his mum stomped back towards the house.

'Oh yeah, it's totally that walk and I think it's also that frown. The one that comes before Mum says "If only you had never let the goats in",' Kerry added. 'Wait for it ...'

Mum slammed the back door.

'Those stinking goats! If only you had never let them in that time, Harry,' she fumed.

'Told you! There it is!' Kerry said, grinning like she'd just won a chocolate cake in a raffle.

4

'That was months ago, Mum, and it was an accident,' Harry protested. 'I was just practising kick-boxing, but because my legs are so long, I accidentally kicked a hole in the fence and the goats got in. How many times do I have to say sorry?'

'A million times? Five million?' Kerry said.

'Be quiet, Kerry,' Mum snapped. 'The point is, Harry, those goats have been breaking into my garden ever since you broke the fence. It was completely irresponsible of you! They are trampling my flower beds, eating my roses and leaving goat droppings all over the place. And I don't like the way they look at me. They've got funny eyes.'

'It's their rectangular pupils,' Harry explained. 'It allows them to see danger approaching from all angles.'

'Like a woman with a pan and a wooden spoon?' Kerry suggested.

Harry laughed and then stopped, quickly, when he saw his mum staring sternly at him.

'Sorry, Mum,' Harry said. 'Sorry for the goats getting in. Sorry for being so tall that I broke the fence. Sorry.'

Harry was eleven, but as tall as a very tall adult. To his friends he was Harry the Hulk, but unlike the actual Hulk, who went green, exploded out of his shirt and smashed things up, Harry was kind and easy-going.

He loved animals (and knew a lot about them).

He loved hanging out with his friends.

He loved muffins and milkshakes.

He loved dressing up in outrageous outfits (and he was pretty good at designing them, too).

Basically, a fancy-dress party with his mates and added penguins, pandas, meerkats and milky drinks was his idea of heaven.

'Where's Mini?' Mum asked, after she had sat down at the kitchen table.

Mini was Harry's granny. Everyone called her Mini. Not Gran or Mum – always Mini.

Unlike Harry, Mini was small, as her nickname suggested. Also unlike Harry, who sometimes felt embarrassed about his height, Mini couldn't have cared less about being short. She marched around like she was the very tiny boss of all things.

'She's in the shower,' said Harry, pointing to the bathroom above with his spoon.

'She's not supposed to be in the shower,' Mum screeched, leaping up. 'No one's supposed to be in the shower. It leaks, remember?'

At that exact moment, a drop of water splashed on Harry's head.

Another bounced off the table.

Then another splashed into Kerry's cereal bowl.

Then – **WHOOSH!** – water began pouring down the walls and streaming out of the light fittings.

Mum raced upstairs.

'Today we can expect sudden downpours in the kitchen,' said Harry, laughing, 'with occasional outbreaks of swearing from Mum. It will be drier later, once Mini gets out of the shower.'

Kerry kicked water at Harry, who laughed

as he dodged out of the way.

Upstairs, Mum was hammering on the bathroom door, roaring at Mini to turn the shower off. But Mini, as well as being small, was slightly deaf. She didn't hear.

More water flooded down. Soon the kitchen floor looked like the shallow end of the leisure centre pool, minus the toddlers in armbands.

Harry and Kerry sprinted upstairs and began pounding on the bathroom door, too. Eventually, the shower went quiet and the door opened.

Mini appeared wearing a fluffy orange dressing gown, her curly white hair hidden beneath a bright pink shower cap.

'Oh, wasn't expecting to find you three standing there,' she said. 'Have you got nothing better to do?'

'You flooded the kitchen, Mini, when you had your shower,' Harry explained. 'It's like a fish pond down there. Or a tiny lake. Or a very big puddle. It's really wet!'

'I see,' said Mini. 'Well, I wouldn't stand around chatting then. You better get downstairs and sort it out.'

CHAPTER TWO

Back in the kitchen, the water had stopped pouring down the walls, but it was now pretty deep. A hamster would have had to do doggy-paddle in it – that's how deep.

'Take these brooms and start sloshing it out of the back door,' said Mum. 'I'll call the plumber.'

Harry and Kerry did as they were told, shunting small tidal waves of water across the kitchen floor and on to the patio outside.

Then Mum appeared in the doorway, frowning.

'The plumber can't come until five p.m. and it's going to take ages to get all this water out,' she said. 'One of you will have to take Mini to the awards.'

'What awards?' asked Harry.

'The Caught Short Awards,' Mum said.

'It's the biggest annual loo-roll award ceremony in the country,' Kerry explained. 'Mini's getting the Lifetime Achievement Award.'

'That's why she's staying with us,' said Mum. 'Keep up, Harry! That's also why I have the day off work. I was going to treat her: take her shopping for a new outfit, take her to the hairdresser's and then go to the awards, but I can't now. Not with all this mess to sort out.'

'Before you ask, I can't do it,' said Kerry. 'I'm going into town with my friends.'

'Harry, you'll have to do it,' said Mum. 'There's no one else.'

'But I'm meeting up with Keith and Jonny and Tom today,' Harry protested. 'I've hardly seen them lately. I've been too busy earning puppy points.'

And ... **STOP!**

Let's just pause the story here for a second, readers, because I've got a feeling you're sitting there thinking, what in the name of savoury waffles are puppy points. Am I right? I knew it. Well, make yourselves comfy and I'll explain. Here we go ...

Harry desperately wanted a dog, but because of his not-great-so-far track record with animals (see the following list of Harry's animal bungles and blunders), Mum didn't believe he was responsible enough to look after a dog.

HARRY'S ANIMAL BUNGLES AND BLUNDERS:

- Breaking the fence while practising kick-boxing so that Primrose and Daisy got in

- Losing the school gerbil under the floorboards for three whole days

- Letting his stick insects escape (they were still showing up all around the house now – in Kerry's sock drawer, on the remote control, swinging on the bathroom light pull)

- Being trampled by
a lamb on a farm visit

- Getting a woodlouse stuck down
his trouser leg

- Having his chips stolen by a
seagull on a trip to the seaside

- Losing control of Uncle Steve's dog, Major
(read on for details)

*So, Mum invented puppy points. Harry could
show how responsible he was by doing
loads of boring jobs around the*

house and earning points for each one.

Jobs like these:

<u>PUPPY POINTS - JOBS</u>

Cleaning the sink - two points

Making all the beds - one point

Vacuuming the stairs - two points

Loading/unloading the dishwasher - one point

Once Harry had earned five hundred points, Mum said he would have proved that he was ready to have his own puppy.

So that's the low-down on puppy points and hopefully that all makes sense now. It does? Wonderful! Let's get back to the story, then.

'Taking Mini to the awards is a good chance for you to earn some more puppy points,' said Mum.

'How many?' Harry asked.

'Let me think ...' said Mum. 'Thirty.'

'What?' shrieked Kerry. 'That's not enough. Harry, stick up for yourself. You've got to take Mini to some awards show that will probably go on for hours, and you're missing out on spending time with your friends. Ask for more points.'

Mum glared at Kerry.

Harry looked a bit worried.

Thirty puppy points was more than he earned in a whole month sometimes. He didn't want to say no to that, but maybe Kerry had a point.

'Fifty?' Harry suggested, unsure.

'Hundred, more like,' said Kerry. 'Ask for a hundred!'

'That's enough, Kerry,' said Mum. 'Fine, Harry, you've got a deal. Fifty puppy points.'

Harry whooped and did a wet, splashy dance.

'But only if you get Mini to the awards, and bring her back here, with her trophy, at the end of the day. Got it?'

'Got it,' said Harry.

'Don't let me down,' said Mum.

'I absolutely won't,' said Harry.

Mum left the kitchen and Harry turned to Kerry.

'Fifty puppy points! This is so awesome! For taking Mini to an awards do, which will be super easy,' he said, flicking her with a wet tea towel.

'Get off!' she yelled, attacking his feet with the broom. 'Why do you want a dog so much anyway?'

'Dogs are great,' said Harry.

'That's it?' said Kerry.

'They're cute and furry and always super excited to see you,' Harry said. 'They have big brown doggy eyes, like chocolate buttons, and soft fur and wet noses. They don't care that I'm super tall for my age. That's just not interesting to them, but they are really smart. I'll be able to train my dog to do tricks like roll over, take my socks off and fetch me a KitKat. My dog will be like a best friend, who's always there and doesn't mind if I'm grumpy or tired. A friend I can watch TV with, even though he won't understand what's going on, and who will keep me company when I'm doing boring homework or off school with a cold.'

'That does sound quite nice,' Kerry admitted.

'Yeah, and I'm going to design cool outfits for my dog, too. I've already drawn sketches for a waterproof, high-visibility reversible coat, with pockets for dog treats. I swear on all the milkshakes from here to Canada, having a dog is going to be brilliant. I'm

totally ready. I just have to convince Mum.'

'How many puppy points have you got already?' Kerry asked.

'Four hundred and twenty-five,' Harry

said. He didn't have to count them. He knew. 'If I get the fifty points today, I'm super close to the target. Only twenty-five to go.'

'Wow, I totally thought you'd never do it,' Kerry said. 'In fact, I thought Mum had set the target deliberately high, hoping you'd give up on the idea.'

'I'd never give up on getting a puppy,' Harry said. **'Not ever.'**

CHAPTER THREE

Harry bounded upstairs to get dressed.

His bedroom walls were covered in posters

of animals, with one wall dedicated to dogs of

all kinds. There were books about animals

piled up, too:

On a hook behind his door, hidden by his school bag, was a little red puppy collar and lead, which Harry had bought with his pocket money.

Harry pulled on black jeans and a matching black T-shirt. Kerry said that when he wore black clothes like this, he looked like a burglar, but Harry thought it stopped him and his massive height from standing out too much.

Back downstairs, Mum handed Harry a card with gold, swirly writing on it.

'This is the invitation,' she said. 'The awards ceremony starts at five p.m. at the Metro Hotel, but you must get there at four

thirty p.m. OK? **DO NOT BE LATE.**
There will be loads of friends and fans there,
all waiting to see Mini get the Lifetime
Achievement Award. They will want selfies
and autographs before the awards start.'

'Fans? Selfies?' Harry said.

'Yes, your gran is a superstar in the world
of loo roll,' said his mum.

'Wow,' said Harry. 'I did not know that.'

Mum then passed him an appointment
card for a salon called Hair Today, Bald
Tomorrow.

'Take Mini here for a haircut at two p.m.,'
Mum said. 'Get some lunch and go to the
department store too. She needs a new outfit.

You can't get a lifetime achievement award while wearing an old cardie. Help her choose something respectable.'

'Whoa, that's lots to do, Harry,' Kerry said. 'Bet you wish you'd asked for one hundred points now.'

'Oh, and don't let Mini eat any toffees,' Mum continued. 'Toffees make her go funny. Never let her out of your sight, either, at any time. She's a fast walker, despite her little legs – remember that – and she sometimes gets "ideas". Don't let her get "ideas".'

'How will I know if she's getting "ideas"?' Harry asked.

'Just keep an eye on her, OK?' Mum said.

'If you can take care of Mini, I might believe you can take care of a dog. So far, the only time I've seen you with a dog was when you looked after Major, Uncle Steve's dog, for the day. He jumped out of the bathroom window and landed right on me. I was enjoying a doze in the sun on my lounger and then, wallop!'

'He was excited about meeting Primrose and Daisy,' Harry explained.

'Then he also ate three pats of butter and threw up under the kitchen table!' said Mum.

'That was actually quite clever, though,' Harry said. 'Not the throwing-up bit, but the fact that he opened the fridge. Very few dogs can do that. Anyway, when it's my own puppy, I'll train it. I promise my dog won't turn out like Major.'

Mini came downstairs and peered into the kitchen.

'Goodness, what a mess ...' she said.

'Yes, and whose fault is that?' Mum snapped.

'Yours, I'd say, seeing as how your shower leaks,' said Mini. 'You want to get that looked at.'

'You weren't supposed to use the shower in the first place!' Mum exploded. 'Why couldn't you have a nice bath instead?'

'Baths are so boring,' said Mini. 'All that

lolling about in hot water. No thanks. Anyway, why did you invite me to stay if your shower wasn't working properly?'

'You're here so we could have a nice day together at the Caught Short Awards, remember?' said Mum. 'I was going to take you out and spoil you. A new outfit, lunch, the hairdresser's. I wanted to choose a hat for you.'

'A hat!' snorted Mini. 'I never wear hats, unless I'm meeting the queen.'

'Have you met the queen?' Harry asked.

'Yes, of course,' said Mini. 'Twice.'

She turned back to Mum.

'I don't want to go to this silly loo-roll

awards thing, let alone dress up for it.'

'You're getting the Lifetime Achievement Award!' said Mum. 'Everyone will be celebrating your life.'

'Yes, looking back at it as if it's over. Well, it isn't,' said Mini firmly. 'There's plenty more I plan to do.'

'There!' said Mum, wagging her finger at Mini. 'Take note, Harry. She's having one of her "ideas". This is how it starts. Watch out for that.'

Harry nodded nervously.

'I'm going to be stuck at home today, sorting out this flood, so Harry will take care of you,' Mum continued.

'I don't need taking care of,' Mini replied. 'I'm seventy-four, not a hundred and four.'

'You have a big day ahead,' said Mum. 'I want you to enjoy it, but you need some support. I don't want you to get tired.'

'I never get tired,' Mini said.

'Have you packed your big red scarf, in case it gets chilly?' Mum said.

'Yes, I've got my scarf,' Mini sighed, rolling her eyes. 'It's in my bag.'

Mini patted the huge bag over her shoulder. Harry looked at it and, not for the first time, wondered what else was in it. He liked to imagine that it contained lots of weird and unexpected things, such as:

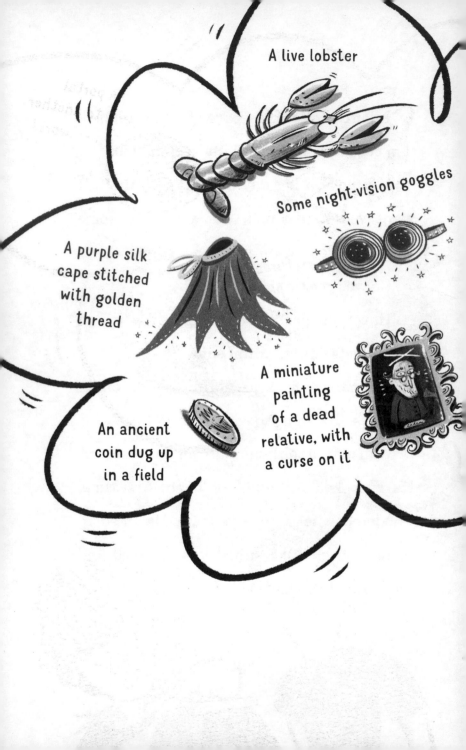

A live lobster

Some night-vision goggles

A purple silk cape stitched with golden thread

A miniature painting of a dead relative, with a curse on it

An ancient coin dug up in a field

'Harry, pay attention,' Mum said, pointing at the open front door, through which Mini had just marched. 'Don't let her out of your sight, remember?'

'Got it,' said Harry. He yanked on his trainers and ran after her.

CHAPTER FOUR

Harry and Mini made an odd couple, walking down the road. Harry the Hulk, tall and lean, all dressed in black, and his white-haired granny, super short, looking completely ordinary apart from a pair of trainers that she liked to describe as 'fresh', and beetling along at a surprisingly rapid pace.

They were heading off in the direction of the town centre, to shop for a new outfit for Mini. Or so Harry thought. But then, unexpectedly, Mini swerved down the road that led to the supermarket.

'Just need to pick up a few things,' she said.

'But what about clothes shopping?' Harry called after her, stopping on the pavement.

Mini didn't hear. She kept going and was soon quite far ahead, nearly at the supermarket car park. Mum had said Mini was a fast walker, but this was way speedier than Harry had imagined. He broke into a jog and had almost caught up with her when a huge delivery lorry pulled out in front of him and slowly rolled past.

By the time it was gone, Mini was nowhere to be seen. How did she do that? Was she on wheels? Did she have a jetpack in her giant bag after all? 'She must be inside already,' Harry muttered to himself. He jogged into the supermarket.

'Would you like to try one of our new goat burgers?' said a lady standing by the entrance. She thrust a tray of tiny burgers in tiny buns towards Harry.

He thought of Primrose and Daisy, and

shuddered. Then he thought of his mum and made a mental note never to tell her that goat burgers were a thing – she might have murderous thoughts.

'No thanks, I'm vegetarian,' said Harry, dodging past her.

Harry glanced around, looking for Mini. Where was she? He decided she must be in the bakery aisle, picking up something for breakfast – not part of the plan, but never mind, he'd soon find her and they'd be back on schedule.

Harry followed the smell of warm bread, past the bagels, the wraps, the pittas and towards the doughnuts.

'Ah, you're nice and tall,' said a voice. Harry looked down. A woman about the same size as Mini, but unfortunately not Mini, was peering up at him.

'I want a cheese scone from that basket at the top, can you reach one for me?' she said.

Harry was frequently asked to do things only tall people could manage – getting Frisbees down out of trees or changing light bulbs, for instance – and people often thought he was much older, which caused confusion. He had been mistaken for a builder (and had to carry a ladder up a street), for a referee at a football match and a mime artist at a local arts festival. A man once thought Harry was a traffic warden, just because he was standing near his car, and pretty much anytime he walked through a cafe, someone assumed he was the waiter and ordered coffee from him.

Harry picked up the tongs and grabbed a scone.

'Too dark,' said the small woman.

'This one?' said Harry.

'Too pale,' said the small woman.

'This one?'

'Too lumpy.'

'This one?'

'Too flat.'

Harry sighed quietly. He didn't have time for 'operation find the perfect cheese scone'.

He was supposed to be taking care of his granny and at this exact moment he didn't even know where she was.

'Maybe this?' said Harry, starting to feel a bit stressed. It was only 9.30 a.m. and he had already lost Mini. Had he blown it? Were those puppy points gone? So soon?

'Ah, yes, that one's fine,' said the woman, finally. She took the scone and trudged away.

'You're welcome,' Harry muttered, and then raced off to search for Mini, diving quickly from aisle to aisle.

Not in the pasta aisle.

Not in the condiments aisle.

Not by the freezers.

Not with the fizzy drinks.

The crisps and snacks aisle was also a Mini-free zone, but when Harry got to the loo rolls, he found a crowd of people. He moved closer and spotted his gran at the centre of it all.

'So excited to meet you,' said a man, grinning madly at Mini. 'Can I get a selfie?'

Mini stared crossly at his phone as he snapped the pic. A woman shook Mini's hand and told her she was 'an inspiration'. Another woman thrust a packet of loo rolls at Mini and begged her to sign them. Mini rummaged around in her huge bag and eventually pulled out a pen and scrawled her name. Then she pointed at Harry.

'Ah, here's my grandson, I have to go.'

'Bet he's not her grandson,' someone in the crowd whispered. 'Bet he's her bodyguard. Look at the size of him!'

Mini pushed past everyone, took Harry by the arm and walked with him towards the exit.

'Handy of you to show up then and help me get away,' she said.

'Of course I showed up,' said Harry. 'I've been looking for you all over the supermarket. I'm taking care of you today, remember?'

'Oh yes, well, as I said to your mother, I don't need taking care of, so you're free to go now, dear,' said Mini. She smiled up at him, a bouncy smile, as her mouth moved up and down as if she was chewing something at the same time.

'I promised Mum I'd stick with you,' Harry said. 'We have to go clothes shopping. Do you need to buy anything here, first of all?'

'No, no, I'm ready to leave,' said Mini. 'I've had enough of all those people making a fuss.'

'They're your fans,' said Harry. 'They really love you.'

'For creating a paper that people use to wipe their bottoms? It's just loo roll! Calm down, everyone,' Mini snorted. 'Come on, let's get out of here.'

CHAPTER FIVE

Mini and Harry walked quickly to the exit, but as soon as they passed through it ...

BEEP, BEEP, BEEP, BEEP.

The alarms sounded, loud and urgent, and a large security guard wearing a high-vis waistcoat appeared.

'Looks like you've forgotten to pay for

something,' he said.

'I don't like your tone,' said Mini to the security guard, giving him a stern look. 'Accusing me of stealing. I'm seventy-four, you know!'

'Just doing my job,' said the security guard.

'Is your job to harass seventy-four-year-old women?' Mini asked. 'Shame on you!'

A couple of shoppers looked over, curious.

'Mini!' Harry hissed. 'Please. Keep your voice down. People are staring.'

'I need to check that there are no unpaid items about your person,' the man said. 'This way, please.'

He steered Mini back towards the self-checkout tills.

'Mini, you shouldn't argue with him, he could have you arrested,' Harry whispered to her.

'No one's going to arrest me, dear,' said Mini. 'They wouldn't dare.'

Then Harry noticed her jaws moving again.

'Wait, you're chewing, aren't you? I thought you were. What are you eating?' he asked. 'It better not be toffees. Mum said you're not allowed to have toffees.'

'What was that? I didn't hear you,' said Mini, pointing at her ears. 'I am quite deaf, you know.'

The security guard stopped next to a till.

'Right, let's see what's inside this giant bag of yours, madam,' he said.

Mini plonked her bag down and began pulling things out.

The big red scarf.

'Unexpected item in the bagging area,' said the till.

A lasso.

'Unexpected item in the bagging area.'

A telescope.

'Unexpected item in the bagging area.'

'See, nothing unusual, Officer,' said Mini. 'Exactly what you'd expect to find in a seventy-four-year-old woman's handbag.'

A whistle on a fluorescent-yellow string.

An egg whisk.

Three mittens.

Gold spray paint.

A tin can labelled Pocket Fog.

A table-tennis bat.

Two chopsticks.

Some kind of small wooden flute.

'What's that?' the security guard asked.

'A pungi,' said Mini. 'They say you can charm snakes with it, but I've never been able to get a decent note out of it.'

'Unexpected item in the bagging area.'

Then Mini pulled out a wad of maps and leaflets for local attractions:

Chesney's Cheese Maze

The Cowpat Museum

Britain's Tiniest Zoo ('Come and Pet our Ladybirds!')

The local theme park, called Fun Valley Adventure Resort.

Next:

A flask of water.

A book about knots.

A penknife.

A postcard of the queen – 'Such a sweetie,'

Mini said, gazing at it for a second.

Then lastly, a homemade pork pie.

'Unexpected item in the bagging area,' the till chanted again and again, until the security guard tapped some buttons to shut it up.

Harry was amazed. He had often dreamed that Mini had crazy things in her huge handbag, and now, right here in the supermarket, he discovered that she actually did.

The security guard looked baffled.

'OK, OK, I've seen enough,' he said. 'You seem to have everything but the kitchen sink in there, but nothing that's stolen.'

'I told you so,' said Mini. 'Now, how about apologising?'

'What?' said the security guard, sounding surprised.

'Mini!' Harry said, blushing the colour of salami.

'Apologise. You know – say sorry,' she repeated.

The security guard fidgeted awkwardly on the spot and rubbed his neck.

'I think the alarm was probably faulty,

that's all,' he said. 'I'll get it checked out.'

'I'm not leaving until you say sorry,' said Mini. 'One little word.'

Harry noticed a crowd of shoppers watching them now, some grinning, some just staring. He cringed and looked at his feet. He hated standing out like this. His cheeks burned even redder, going from salami to tandoori chicken.

The security guard was quiet for a moment, then muttered, 'Sorry.'

'Tiny bit louder,' said Mini. 'I am quite deaf, you know.'

'Sorry,' said the security guard, louder this time.

'There we are,' said Mini. 'Wasn't so hard, was it?'

Mini tumbled all her stuff back into her bag and trotted towards the exit with the security guard trailing sheepishly behind.

Harry followed, still painfully aware of people staring at him and wishing he could magically shrink down to the size of a beetle and skitter away. Fat chance. Harry's height made him super visible, like a giraffe surrounded by zebras. All he could do was put his head down and will his cheeks to go from tandoori chicken to a less bright shade. Maybe ham? Or even salmon?

At the exit, Mini turned and shook the

security guard's hand.

'Better luck next time,' she said, and then Harry noticed something. A look in Mini's eye. No, not a look, a twinkle. A definite twinkle. Was she having one of her 'ideas' that Mum had warned him about? Then she bombed through the doors, as fast as her size-three trainers would carry her, and ...

BEEP, BEEP, BEEP, BEEP.

The security alarms shrieked into life.

'Hey, get back here,' shouted the security guard.

'Mini!' shouted Harry. 'You've been eating toffees, haven't you? Stolen toffees? I knew it!'

Mini whipped a packet of toffees out of her

coat pocket and waved them in the air gleefully, but she didn't stop. She was off, speeding through the car park, with the security guard running behind.

Harry followed, too shocked to care about people staring at him now. He was supposed to be spending the day with his granny, but already – this! She was on the run!

As Harry raced to catch up, he saw Mini reach into her bag and pull out the lasso. No! What? She wasn't going to … ? She wouldn't dare … ? Did she even know … ?

Harry watched, hand over his mouth, as Mini whirled the lasso round and round above her head and let it fly.

It looped perfectly
around a trolley, which,
with one flick, Mini
sent spinning into
the security guard's
path.

'Where did she learn to do that?'

Harry gasped as the security guard tumbled and stumbled and then heaved the trolley out of the way, and started running after her again.

Mini, still moving fast, reached into her bag again and this time ...

Something solid and brown flew through the air and bounced off the security guard's head.

OOF!

He stopped in his tracks, clutching his forehead.

'That wasn't the pork pie, was it?' Harry said. He spotted a large chunk of pastry stuck to the security guard's right eyebrow. By all the muffins of Tuesday! It *was* the pork pie.

Harry pulled his eyes away from the security guard, who was wiping his forehead with a hanky, and turned to look for his granny. Where was she now? He glanced this way and that, and then saw a small figure with bright white hair.

The figure was no longer running, though.

It was standing on the back of the huge delivery lorry Harry had seen on his way in. It was holding on to its rear doors with one hand and waving with the other as the lorry swooped out of the car park and drove away.

'Mini!' Harry yelled. 'Come back!'

No chance. She was gone.

CHAPTER SIX

Harry checked his watch: 10.30 a.m. He had only left the house an hour ago and already he had lost his granny.

She had stolen toffees from the supermarket.

She had pork-pied a security guard.

She had escaped on the back of a lorry.

This was not the way to win fifty puppy points.

'I have to find her,' Harry muttered, but he had no idea where to start. The lorry could be miles away now. He decided to run back into town and check the park.

Grans like parks, don't they?

Not this one. There was no sign of her.

Harry popped into the cafe, where Bruce, the owner, was buttering a tower of white bread slices.

'Have you seen my granny?' Harry asked. 'Did she come in for breakfast?'

'These are the only customers I've had today,' Bruce replied, pointing at a table of

five nuns. The nuns looked round and waved
at Bruce.

'The sisters love their bacon sandwiches,'
Bruce said, waving back.

Harry went outside again and, unsure

what to do, sat down on a bench to think. Where could Mini be?

'You're late,' said a familiar voice. It was Keith.

'Yes, you are late,' said Jonny and Tom, standing next to him – all Harry's friends. They had been waiting for him to arrive.

'It's because of my granny,' blurted Harry. 'I've got to find her. I'm supposed to get her to an awards do starting at four thirty p.m.'

'But we are meant to be hanging out today,' said Tom.

'I know, I know,' said Harry. 'Things have changed. Sorry. My mum said I could have fifty puppy points if I looked after my granny today, but she disappeared on the back of a lorry and now I've lost her.'

'Oh yeah, still saving up for a puppy,' Jonny said. 'Do you never give up on that?'

'No, why would I?' said Harry.

Keith took the pump off his bike, put it into his armpit and slowly pushed air in, creating a whistling sound that ended in a ripply grunt.

'Have you tried calling her?' Keith suggested.

'She doesn't have a mobile phone,' Harry said. 'She's got a lot of stuff in her handbag, that's for sure, but not a phone.'

Harry put his head in his hands.

'I can't believe I've lost Mini,' he sighed. 'The exact opposite of what I was supposed to do.'

'You haven't lost her,' said Tom. 'She chose to disappear. It's not your fault. She's doing what she wants, which is fine. She's a grown-up woman.'

'A very small grown-up woman,' Harry said.

'You know what I mean,' said Tom. 'She's an adult. She can take care of herself.'

'I promised Mum, though,' said Harry. 'And fifty puppy points is loads if I can pull it off. Then it's only twenty-five to go. I could have a dog by the end of the summer holidays.'

Keith pumped more air into his armpit, producing a wave of guffy ripples.

'I just need to find her, but how?' Harry asked.

'Simple,' said Keith. 'I've watched enough episodes of *Meet & Tuveg*, the best detective show ever, to know that when you have a missing person, you don't run about all over town in a panic. You think. You get into the mind of the person you're tracking. Build a character profile. What kind of person is your granny?'

'A granny sort of person,' said Harry.

'Small.

White hair.

Bit deaf.

Seventy-four.

Used to work with loo roll.

Flooded the kitchen by having a shower when she knew the shower was leaky.

Just stole a bag of toffees from the supermarket.'

'So all that tells you she doesn't play by the rules,' said Keith. 'She does things her way. This is good.'

'Is it?' Harry asked.

'Now, think about where she might go,' Keith continued. 'Where has she always wanted to go? Where would she feel happy?'

Harry thought hard. Mini hadn't wanted to go and buy a new outfit, she wanted to go to the supermarket for toffees that she wasn't supposed to eat and didn't pay for. Then she escaped on a lorry. This was quite full-on.

Suddenly, it seemed obvious that going to a garden centre or the bingo would not be top of Mini's list. Too boring. She'd want to go somewhere far more exciting.

Then Harry remembered the fliers for local attractions that Mini had in her bag, including one for the theme park on the edge of town.

'Fun Valley Adventure Resort! Oh, thundering crumpets! That's it,' Harry said. 'Keith, you're a genius!'

'You could be right there,' said Keith.

'Can I borrow your bike?'

'No,' said Keith.

Harry jumped on it and pedalled away.

CHAPTER SEVEN

Keith's bike was too small for Harry, and so he had to cycle hunched up over the handlebars, his knees bouncing up around his chest, like a dad messing about on his toddler's trike at a barbecue. That's why, about thirty minutes later, when Harry arrived at Fun Valley Adventure Resort, he was out of breath and hot. His face was glowing red like a tomato on a sunbed. His back was aching.

Harry hid the bike behind a bin and then walked towards the ticket gates. He joined the queue and peered into the theme park. He saw people milling about and lots of children, yanking their parents' hands, desperate to get on a ride, but he couldn't see his granny. There were also two people dressed up in big foam costumes. One looked like a bag of chips, another a sausage. They were the characters from the popular cartoon *Sausage & Chips*. They were greeting people and handing out balloons.

The queue moved forwards. Harry squinted and stared over people's heads, looking for his tiny granny. No sign. As he got nearer to the ticket booth, he noticed that people were paying for their entry passes. Of course they were. But then again, uh-oh! Harry patted his pockets. Empty. He had no money. How was he going to get in?

Then he had an idea.

'I'm here to work, dressing up like them,' said Harry, pointing at Sausage and Chips. 'They said come to the main gates and you would tell me where to go.'

'Ah right, costumed entertainment,' said the man on the ticket desk. 'You'll be perfect –

nice and tall. The props department is round to the right. Follow the signs saying **STAFF ONLY**. Have fun.'

That was that. The gate opened and Harry walked through. Simple. He couldn't believe his lie had worked. He couldn't believe he had lied at all.

Now, to find his granny.

Harry looked around. Giant roller coasters and plunging rides stood out against the skyline. The park stretched far into the distance, peppered with trees, shops and food stalls. How on earth would he locate Mini here?

'Looking for the props department, aren't you?' said a voice behind him. It was the man from the ticket booth. 'I'll take you. I'm going that way myself.'

'I, um ...'

It was no use. The ticket man strode off, calling over his shoulder, 'Come on, this way.'

Harry obediently followed him, feeling panic bubble in his belly. 'Have to find Mini, have to find Mini, have to find Mini ...' was playing on a loop in his brain, but the loop stopped abruptly when Harry found himself inside the props department, a warehouse on the edge of the park. Inside, every kind of man-sized costume hung from rails:

Bears and chickens.

Fairies and cavemen.

Chocolate bars.

Dragons.

Hot dogs.

A giant Planet Earth.

Harry gazed at all the costumes, amazed. It was like he'd walked out of real life and into a fantasy world – *his* fantasy world, where people could dress up as hot dogs and dragons whenever they pleased.

'This young man is here to work on costumed entertainment today,' said the ticket barrier guy.

'Excellent,' said a friendly-looking woman wearing huge glasses with red frames. 'I'm Liz. Welcome to my world of costumes! We need Cheesehead the Chipmunk to walk around today. Just wave, greet children, stop for photos. That kind of thing. Take your trainers off, you won't need those.'

Liz heaved an enormous furry suit off a rail. The chipmunk was made of golden fur, with a fluffy tail. It wore a red bow tie and giant red shoes. In one hand, it held a big wedge of cheese.

Liz undid the zip at the back and Harry climbed in, wondering how his day had spun so out of control that he had not only lost his granny – the one thing he was supposed not to do – but was now dressing up as a chipmunk at a theme park.

On any other day, the chance to wear a giant costume would have been a dream come true for Harry, but not today, not today ...

Liz grabbed the big chipmunk head and pushed it on over Harry's head. It felt heavy and smelt faintly of school changing rooms. He couldn't hear very well and he had to look out of its mouth.

'Here are some Chipmunk Chunks to give to children,' said Liz, handing Harry some sweeties in shiny wrappers. 'You can store them in your pouch.'

'Chipmunks don't have pouches. They're rodents, not marsupials,' Harry said, but his words were muffled inside the huge head.

Liz steered him towards the door and, with a gentle shove on his furry chipmunk back, pushed him out into the theme park.

'Have fun!' she said.

CHAPTER EIGHT

Harry began to walk, but it wasn't easy. The first problem was the shoes. They were huge and clumsy, like Harry had sheep sitting on his feet. He couldn't walk in the usual left-right, left-right way. Instead, he had to pick his feet up, as if he were escaping a snowdrift, or pretending to walk on the moon.

The second problem was the chipmunk head, which was mostly foam and had such a small window to look out of that Harry felt he was squinting through a letter box. That's why, almost immediately, he bumped into a signpost, kicked a sparrow, squashed an entire family of ants crossing in front of him and knocked over a bin.

Harry lumbered onwards, despite his feet and head issues, but then some children ran over and began punching him in his tummy and standing on his giant red shoes, laughing and calling him 'a fat mouse-thing'.

He struggled to balance as he reached into his pouch and threw some Chipmunk Chunks out. The children rushed to gather them up, then ran back to their families, holding up their sweetie treasure.

Puffed and hot, Harry began moving again. He needed to hurry. He had to find his granny. What time was it now? He didn't know. His watch was hidden under the furry costume. By now Mini could be anywhere.

Gradually, Harry got into a rhythm with his giant feet and, ignoring people's requests for photos, lolloped through the theme park.

He passed the Tiddly Teacups and the Happy Caterpillar Train and scanned the crowds queuing for the Crazy Commotion ride and Barf Mountain – no sign of Mini.

Then something caught his eye in the distance. A flash of white on the Big Drop. The white of white curly hair? Could it be? Was it? Mini? Mini?

Harry moved towards the ride. People were getting off it now and standing around near the exit, looking queasy. Was that her, there, in the crowd? Harry wasn't sure.

POPCORN

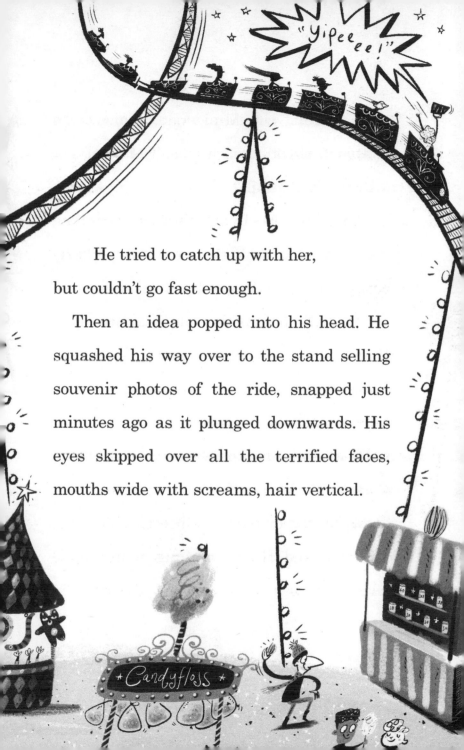

"Yipeeee!"

He tried to catch up with her,
but couldn't go fast enough.

Then an idea popped into his head. He
squashed his way over to the stand selling
souvenir photos of the ride, snapped just
minutes ago as it plunged downwards. His
eyes skipped over all the terrified faces,
mouths wide with screams, hair vertical.

Candyfloss

'Not Mini, not Mini, not Mini …' he muttered, checking each face. 'Not Mini, not Mini. Wait … Mini!'

There she was. In the first car. Grinning from ear to ear. White hair still perfectly curled. Giant handbag gripped on her lap.

'That was her on the ride. I did see her!' Harry said. 'She must be nearby.'

He plodded off, full of determination.

He would find his granny.

He would get her to the awards on time.

He would win the fifty puppy points.

'Make way, excuse me, Cheesehead coming through,' said Harry, barging people aside with his big belly.

Where would Mini go next? She'd done the Big Drop, so what now? He heard screams above. Tipping his heavy chipmunk head back, he looked up through its mouth and saw the park's biggest and scariest roller coaster, the Upside Downer, threading overhead. People were hanging completely upside down in their cars as they zipped over the crowds below.

'Ah yes …' Harry muttered. 'That one.'

Harry was beginning to get into the mind of his granny now, just as Keith had recommended, just as Meet and Tuveg the detectives would do.

He had thought Mini was a regular no-dramas granny, but since the supermarket, he had begun to see her true personality. She was daring, cheeky and definitely a rule breaker.

It wasn't too far to the Upside Downer, but the crowds were thick and the going would be slow. What to do? Harry looked around and realised that the quickest route was straight through the wallaby enclosure in the animal park. He scoped it out. Over the fence – yup, he was tall enough to clear it – a short walk and then, **BADING! BADONG!** He could be right by the ride in moments, find Mini and get the day back on track.

Harry cleared the fence easily. A few wallabies looked up. Maybe they thought, Oh look, a giant chipmunk wearing red shoes and a bow tie is in our enclosure. Then again, maybe they didn't.

Harry nodded politely at the wallabies and then broke into a blobby run. He was almost at the opposite fence when his giant red shoe got tangled on a tree branch lying on the ground and – **BAM!** – he fell, face first, on to the grass. For a few seconds, he worried he might be stuck there, forever, the extreme fatness of his costume making it impossible to move, let alone find his granny. But then Harry began to wriggle, to heave and pitch, like a ship in stormy seas, and eventually he managed to roll over.

When he looked up, he could see not the sky but a wallaby.

'Hello,' he said as it sniffed his huge foam head. 'Now, you're a real marsupial, aren't you, with a real pouch. Not like this chipmunk. I'm not really a chipmunk, by the way. This is just a costume. I'm Harry.'

The wallaby didn't reply. It hopped out of view and then a human face appeared. It was the wallaby keeper.

'You all right in there?' he asked, peering down at Harry.

'Bit stuck actually, my suit is really heavy,' Harry said.

'Let me help you,' said the keeper, hooking his arm under Harry's and pulling him to his feet.

'Thanks,' said Harry, once he was upright again.

'No problem,' said the keeper. 'You've made my day. A giant squirrel in the wallaby enclosure. Never seen that before. Magic!'

CHAPTER NINE

As Harry got closer to the Upside Downer, he could hear an argument. One of the voices was very familiar. Mini's.

'What do you mean I can't go on the ride?'

'You're too short, I'm afraid,' came the reply. 'There's a height restriction on this ride.'

'I'm not a child. I'm seventy-four, you know!'

'Mini!' Harry shouted. He could see her now, but she didn't notice him. She was too busy lecturing the man at the ride entrance.

'I've just been on the Big Drop and I was fine,' she said. 'Some people were practically wetting their pants, but I loved it. So don't tell me I can't go on the Upside Downer.'

'It's nothing to do with how scared you might be,' replied the man. 'It's purely to do with your height. You're too small. You might slip out of the car when it flips upside down.'

Mini snorted in disbelief.

Harry pushed to the front of the crowd,

shouting, 'Security, stand aside,' and took Mini by the arm.

'Security, please come with me, madam,' he said.

'Since when do security guards dress up as weasels?' she said.

'I'm a chipmunk, actually,' he said.

'Chipmunks don't have pouches!' said Mini.

'I know,' said Harry, 'but I can't get into that now. Look, just come over here, please.'

He led Mini away from the crowds.

'Now, can you help me pull my head off? I've only got one free hand, the other one's holding this piece of cheese,' he said.

Harry knelt down so Mini could reach the Velcro fastening. She ripped it open and then lifted the chipmunk head off.

'Oh, it's you, Harry. What are you doing here, dear?' Mini asked.

'Looking for you, of course!' Harry said.

'There's no need to do that,' said Mini. 'I'm perfectly happy and having a nice time. Isn't there something else you'd rather be doing?'

'But I promised I'd take care of you,' said Harry, fanning his hot face.

Mini reached in her bag and gave him her flask of water, which he glugged down in one.

'Toffee?' she said, offering him the bag. Harry shook his head angrily.

'No thanks. I don't eat stolen food,' he said.

'Suit yourself,' said Mini. She put them away, and then pulled a packet of spicy crisps out of her bag, which she began eating.

'Seriously Spicy Extra Red Hot Chips?' Harry spluttered. 'They're the hottest, spiciest crisps in the world! Since when do you eat spicy food?'

'Since my time living in Mexico, thirty years ago. I was working on a secret project there,' said Mini, winking. 'I haven't always been in loo roll.'

Spicy food!

Secret projects!

Mexico!

Harry could hardly take in all this new granny info.

'Wow, it's her,' said a man, pointing at Mini. He rushed over and stood next to her, beaming.

'Please, could I get a photo with you?' he asked. 'You're the absolute goddess of loo rolls. I'm a huge admirer of your work.'

Mini batted his words away, like she was swatting midges, but allowed him to snap a photo and then squeezed out a smile before he walked away.

'Wow, another fan,' Harry said. 'We haven't even made it to the awards yet. In fact, we should get going. We have to choose a new outfit, remember? And I'm taking you to lunch and then you have the hairdresser's at two p.m.'

Then Harry felt a tap on his shoulder. It was a giant banana.

'Never take your head off when you're working on costumed entertainment,' the giant banana said. 'It's the law. It destroys the illusion that you're a real chipmunk.'

'A real chipmunk? With a pouch! Ha!' Mini said.

'I'm in a costume by mistake,' said Harry. 'This is my granny. I just need to get her to come with me …'

Harry couldn't see the expression on the person's face, but whoever was inside the giant banana shrugged.

'Look, mate, I don't know what you're up to, but I do know you should keep your head on – your chipmunk head, that is – when you're in the park. First rule of costumed entertainment – never reveal your true identity. It ruins the magic for the kiddies.'

The giant banana then grabbed the

chipmunk head and brought it down firmly on to Harry's head, Velcroing it in place. Harry spluttered and wobbled, and by the time he had adjusted it, so the mouth window lined up with his eyes, Mini was already halfway across the park and heading for the exit.

Not again!

She was on the run – literally – and yet again, moving incredibly fast. Did she never get tired?

There was nothing for it – Harry had to follow her. Don't let her out of your sight, his mum had said. Oh, how simple that had sounded this morning.

Harry took off after her, using his giant belly like a snowplough, scattering small children to left and right. He saw Mini bomb out of the exit and hurry through the picnic area beyond.

Harry felt his face heating up again; he felt his cheeks going tandoori chicken red again – not from embarrassment this time but from the rising temperature inside his chipmunk head. He reached round to the Velcro fastening at the back, grappling with it, hoping to get the volcano-hot head off.

'Gah!' he puffed. 'Can't do it!'

Never mind. It would have to stay on. The thing that mattered – the only thing – was to find Mini. But where was she?

Harry had made it through the picnic area, dodging clumsily around tables, and was out on the street now. He peered through the chipmunk's mouth. Cars everywhere, and a bus coming. It pulled into a stop up the road – there! That telltale flash of Mini's white hair bobbed on to it. The doors closed. It was off.

'Right!' said Harry. 'I see you, Mini. You won't get away this time.'

CHAPTER TEN

Harry grabbed Keith's bike, still hidden behind the bin, and began pedalling after the bus.

If riding Keith's too-small bike had been hard before, it was almost impossible now that Harry was dressed as a chipmunk. His red foam feet could hardly feel the pedals. It was like when you're wearing six pairs of thermal socks and can't tell that you've stepped on some Lego. His legs had to splay out to the sides to make room for his chipmunk belly too, which butted up against the handlebars like a furry airbag.

Harry pedalled past some builders eating sausage rolls at the side of the road. They laughed at him and shouted, 'Look at that giant rat on a bike.'

'Chipmunk,' Harry muttered, but there was no time to stop and explain. Cars passed him, tooting their horns and flashing their lights. A group of teenage girls snapped photos of him on their phones.

Harry tried to keep the bus within sight. He was panting hard now and his hot breath was collecting inside his chipmunk head, pushing the temperature higher and higher. When would Mini get off?

Eventually, the bus slowed at a stop near the clock tower in the centre of town and Harry spotted his granny hopping off.

He glanced up at the big clock: 12.40 p.m. Could she actually be heading to the department store to find a new outfit for the awards? It would be great if she were, but Harry suspected that no, she wouldn't do that. He had learned a lot about his granny today and one thing he now knew for sure was that she hardly ever did what she was supposed to.

He was right. He saw her trotting off, not towards the shops, but in the opposite direction, towards the leisure centre. Harry quickly shoved Keith's bike into a rack and followed her.

He was so focused on keeping his tiny granny in his sights that he wasn't aware of what else was going on around him and, just as he was gaining on her, someone grabbed his chipmunk arm and spun him round.

'Brilliant. Love the costume, that's so great.'

Harry looked down. A woman was smiling up at him, surrounded by a crowd of people. Behind them, there was a stand with a big sign saying Happy Rodent Awareness Day. People were shaking collection tins – Raising Money for a Rodent Play Park – and handing out rodent fact sheets, which said things like, 'Did you know beavers are rodents too?'

'This is totally inspired,' said the woman. 'We really need people to see the good in rodents. Dressing up like this will definitely help. It's just so fun! Great job!'

Now, other Rodent Awareness Day people came to shake Harry's one free chipmunk hand (the one not holding a piece of cheese), and congratulate him on his amazing costume.

'I'm just trying to find my granny,' Harry muttered. 'Really, I have to go. Sorry.'

No good. He was surrounded now by excited Rodent Awareness Day folk, patting and hugging him.

'Please, I must catch up with my granny,' Harry said, but his protests were muffled inside his giant chipmunk head. Nobody heard a word.

'Love the mascot,' said a photographer from the local paper, pointing at Harry. He asked all the Rodent Awareness Day people to line up, with Harry in the middle, and he began taking photos.

'Can you give me a thumbs up?' said the photographer. 'You, the fella in the raccoon suit.'

Harry raised a thumb reluctantly.

'Maybe do a little dance?' the photographer suggested.

'Really, I have to go ...'

Again, no one heard. Harry felt a trickle of sweat dribble down his face as he shook his head. Everyone began chanting, 'Dance, dance, dance, dance.'

'Come on, mate, just give it a little shimmy,'

said the photographer, his massive camera lens pointed right at Harry.

There was nothing else for it ... Harry wiggled his squishy tummy and bobbed his head. The crowd laughed and whooped and began dancing alongside him. The photographer kept shouting 'lovely' and 'nice' as he took more photos, and passers-by stopped to watch.

This is so embarrassing, Harry thought, so deeply, deeply embarrassing. Then he remembered: At least no one knows who I am. They can't see my face.

With this reassuring thought in his head, Harry continued to dance, and with each step and shimmy, he slowly but purposefully wiggled and waggled his way towards the edge of the group of Rodent Awareness Day folk, until he could finally break into a plodding run, in the direction of the leisure centre.

When the Rodent Awareness Day people realised that Harry had scarpered, they called out, 'Hey, come back, don't you want to stay for the competition later? The rodent who looks most like its owner. You can be judge.'

But Harry didn't stop. And he didn't look back.

CHAPTER ELEVEN

Harry pushed open the door to the leisure centre, tripping over his feet as he went. He could feel sweat trickling down his back now, as though his head were actually melting. He cursed the chipmunk suit.

If I designed a chipmunk suit, I'd use lighter-weight padding, he thought, and add some vents under the arms. An easy-access zip too, so the wearer can take it off without help. And no pouch! Who ever saw a chipmunk with a pouch?

A little boy choosing chocolate from the vending machine turned and pointed at Harry.

'Meerkat!' he shouted.

'Not even close, mate,' Harry muttered, and then walked up to reception, where a woman with a name badge that said 'Beverly' was sitting.

'Oh, hello. Good outfit,' said Beverly. 'I love hamsters. So cute.'

'It's a chipmunk, actually,' said Harry.

'Hamsters don't have furry tails. Or pouches. Well, they have pouches in their cheeks, for storing food, but not this kind.'

He patted his belly.

'Then again, neither do chipmunks. Have pouches, that is.'

Beverly looked confused, then shrugged and said, 'How can I help you?'

Harry remembered again that he had no money. How was he going to get in?

Then he remembered how he'd lied to get into Fun Valley Adventure Resort. Lying was not something he liked to do. He was usually one hundred per cent honest, but today was not a usual sort of day and so, thinking fast, he said, 'I'm the mascot for the, er, basketball game. They're expecting me.'

Beverly squinted at her computer screen.

'There's a netball game starting at three, but no basketball ...'

'Netball! Yes, netball! That's it,' said Harry. He glanced at the clock – 1.10 p.m.

'I'm early,' he said. 'It's good to be early, isn't it?'

Beverly shrugged again and waved Harry through.

'Before I go, would you help me take my head off, please?' Harry asked. 'My chipmunk head, I mean.'

Beverly undid the Velcro fastening at the back and pulled the chipmunk head off. Harry took a huge breath, like he'd been held under water for ages.

'Oh wow, that feels good,' he said. 'Thanks, Beverly. Here, have a Chipmunk Chunk.'

Harry handed Beverly a sweetie and then lumbered off to find his granny. He still couldn't move very fast, but with the chipmunk head off, he could at least see and breathe easily and he didn't feel as though his cheeks were going to burst into flames.

Harry checked the leisure centre cafe first, but Mini wasn't there. She wasn't in the gym, on the badminton courts, playing ping-pong or doing a jazz yoga class. Harry half expected her to be in the boxing ring, thumping a huge punchbag, but she wasn't there either.

That panicky feeling, by now quite familiar, fluttered in his belly again like moths round a street light as Harry, finally, checked the swimming pool. He stood at the spectators' window and peered down. An old man was doing the breaststroke, like a slow-motion turtle. The only other person around was the lifeguard, sitting on a high chair overlooking the water. He glanced at her. Then did a double take. The lifeguard was small, with curly white hair.

'Mini!' he gasped.

Harry rubbed his eyes.
Yes, he had seen right. Yes,
it was Mini, wearing the
yellow-and-red leisure centre
shorts and T-shirt, and with
the whistle that had been in
her bag now around her
neck.

Thousands of questions
crowded into Harry's brain.
How long had his gran
been a lifeguard?

Could she do the backstroke? And the front crawl? Did the chlorine in the pool make her hair feel dry? Could she swim with trainers on? Could she hold her breath for as long as a sea otter (five minutes)?

Harry was about to clatter down to the pool and confront her when he caught sight of himself in the glass of the window. He looked ridiculous. His hair was slick with sweat, his face bright red like furious ketchup, and he was still dressed as a chipmunk from the neck down. There was no way he wanted to go to the awards ceremony looking like this. Perhaps he didn't have to.

'How long do lifeguard shifts last?' he

asked Beverly, back at reception.

'At least an hour,' she replied.

'Fantastic, thank you,' said Harry, heading for the changing rooms. Mini could only be a little way through her shift, which meant he had time.

Time to change out of this stupid furry costume.

Time to run home and put on some clean clothes.

Time to get back and grab his granny just as she finished lifeguarding.

She wouldn't get away again!

CHAPTER TWELVE

Harry waddled into the changing rooms, squeezed himself into a cubicle and put the chipmunk head down on the bench. He began fumbling for the zip at the back of the costume with his one free hand (the one not holding a piece of cheese), but because it was a fat foam chipmunk hand, he could hardly feel anything through it. It was like trying to pick up a raisin while wearing boxing gloves.

Harry wriggled and stretched, reaching over his shoulder, round his ribs, up his spine, trying to get at the zip. He looked like he was doing a one-armed exercise class, or an ancient rain dance, or performing an airport security pat-down on himself. He strained and lunged, his fat chipmunk body banging and thumping against the sides of the cubicle, making it shake, but nothing worked.

Next, Harry tried jumping up and down, hoping that might jiggle the zip open. It didn't. Then he searched all over the suit – between his legs, under his arms – for some kind of emergency exit, escape hatch or ejector seat. Had the designer not installed one? No. There was nothing. He was totally and utterly trapped inside a giant foam-and-fur chipmunk.

He began to feel desperate. He wanted the suit off – now! Right now! He couldn't stand to wear it a moment longer. Still wriggling to reach the zip, Harry felt his breathing speed up, his eyes narrow and then, suddenly, the quiet, gentle Harry snapped like a matchstick and his nickname – Harry the Hulk – burst out.

'GET! THIS! THING! OFF! ME!' he bellowed and, with one giant heave,

he ripped Cheesehead the Chipmunk in two.
There was a loud tearing sound. Stuffing
rose up into the air like clouds. Chipmunk
Chunks tumbled to the floor. Then, panting,
Harry stepped clean of the suit, feeling the
cool air on his body for the first time in
hours. He kicked the stupid huge shoes off
his feet – and then froze.

Staring up at him from the floor was a
small, furry animal, with long ears, long
back legs and tiny arms. Harry gasped.

'A wallaby!' he whispered. 'What
in the name of croissants ... ?
Hang about.

Did you crawl into my pouch when I fell over in your enclosure at the theme park?'

Harry bent down and tickled the baby wallaby on its furry cheek. It nuzzled into Harry's hand. He scooped it up and cuddled it. It licked his chin.

'You're very gorgeous,' cooed Harry, immediately transported to that warm, happy place he always went to when he was around animals. 'What lovely ears, and you've got a proper pouch, haven't you?'

Then he remembered – he had a job to do.

He checked his watch: 1.20 p.m. Just over three hours to go until the awards started, and still so much to do.

'You'll have to come with me, little one,' Harry said, and he opened the changing-room door. A little boy was standing outside.

'Is that a kangaroo?' he asked.

'No, it's a wallaby,' Harry said.

'Are you its dad?'

'No, I'm only eleven,' said Harry.

The boy shrugged.

Harry hid the baby wallaby inside his T-shirt and made for the exit, feeling the wet changing-room-floor tiles against his bare feet. Then he remembered that he had taken his trainers off when he'd changed into Cheesehead at the theme park. He had no shoes.

Luckily, just outside were shoes in abundance, neatly lined up under benches, where people sat to take them off before going into the changing rooms.

Harry hurriedly looked for something his size, and found a pair of big blue flip-flops. He put them on and made for the exit. The flip-flops slapped against the tiled floor, sounding like a seal clapping at a fireworks display, but Harry hardly noticed. He was too delighted with how light and fast he felt, now that he was finally free of the chipmunk costume. It was **amazing, incredible!** He felt like a unicorn with wings, or a cheetah on an electric scooter. He could probably run across water or up the side of a skyscraper, he decided. That's how light and fast he felt.

With a gleeful **'whoop!'**, Harry vaulted the turnstile at reception (Beverly was too busy chewing a Chipmunk Chunk to say anything), and then, cradling the wallaby against his belly, he ran down the road.

Harry was home in no time. He tiptoed round the side of his house and peeped into the kitchen window. His mum was there, still mopping up the flood. He glanced at his watch: 1.30 p.m. If Mini's shift had started around 1 p.m. and lasted an hour, then she'd finish at 2 p.m. He had half an hour to get inside, get changed and get back to the leisure centre.

The only problem was, he wasn't supposed to be at home. This was not included on the day's schedule. If his mum saw him she'd explode like a stick of dynamite. Those puppy points would be toast. Could he creep inside without her spotting him, like a ninja burglar, or a very quiet spy? No, he decided, he was too big and clumsy to pull that off. He would have to create a distraction instead. But what?

A bleating noise came from next door's garden.

'Of course,' Harry murmured. 'Primrose and Daisy.'

CHAPTER THIRTEEN

Harry crept quietly into the garden and crawled towards the fence. Mr Hoof, the neighbour, had nailed a plank over the hole the goats had squeezed through that morning, but there was a small gap. Harry peeped through.

'Primrose! Daisy!' he whispered. 'Come

over here. Quick!'

They ignored him. Then Harry spotted some pants on the washing line. He poked them through the fence.

'Delicious pants, yum, yum, yum.'

Primrose trotted over and tugged at them.

'If you want them, come and get them,' he said.

Harry yanked the pants through the gap and scooted back to the side of the house, then waited. It didn't take long.

There was a loud cracking sound. Primrose had butted the fence. A few more thumps and then – **wallop!** – she arrived with a triumphant bleat in Harry's garden. Daisy squeezed through the hole after her.

'You beauties,' Harry said. He loved those goats. He loved them even more when they trotted over to the washing line and began plucking pants off it, like they were picking raspberries.

Seconds later, the back door opened and Harry saw his mum (aka Pan Woman—Goat Nemesis) rush outside, shrieking, 'Get off my knickers, you horrible creatures!'

Harry felt sorry for Primrose and Daisy. They were going to get yelled at again by his mum, just so that he could creep into the house unnoticed, but then he saw Daisy kicking over a garden chair and Primrose tossing a pair of pink pants into the air with her tiny goat horns, and realised they could take care of themselves.

Harry sped round to the front door, snuck inside and took the stairs three at a time with his long legs. He dashed into his bedroom, put the wallaby on his bed, then zoomed into the bathroom for a quick wash.

Back in his room, Harry changed into a bright white top with a bold 'H' for Harry on the front. The dark colours that he usually wore to help his tallness blend in didn't seem that necessary any more. He had just spent several hours dressed as a giant chipmunk, for goodness sake. Wearing colourful clothes would be nothing compared to that. He pulled on some trainers and looked at the wallaby on his bed.

'What can I carry you in?' Harry said. A pillowcase would be pouch-like, but he needed something with handles. His backpack looked too rigid. He snuck into Kerry's room to see if she had something and ...

'What the heck are you doing here?' she yelled at him.

Harry jumped with shock. Kerry was lying on her bed, eating biscuits.

'What are *you* doing here?' he asked. 'You're supposed to be in town with friends.'

'They cancelled,' Kerry said.

'Cancelled?' Harry said. 'When do your friends ever cancel going into town? That's all they ever do.'

Kerry shrugged.

'Oh, I get it,' said Harry. 'They didn't cancel because you never had a plan to go into town with them at all. That was just a handy lie to get you out of taking care of Mini for the day.'

'Well, it doesn't matter,' said Kerry. 'You wanted the puppy points. Anyway, where is Mini and why are you here? Shouldn't you be with her?'

Harry rubbed his head with his knuckles, feeling tiredness break over him like a wave. He sat down heavily on Kerry's bed.

'Taking care of Mini is really difficult,' said Harry. 'She keeps running off. I lost her in the supermarket and then again at the theme park.'

'She was never meant to be at the supermarket or the theme park, was she?' Kerry asked.

'No, she wasn't,' said Harry. 'Now she's at the leisure centre. Did you know she works as a lifeguard? And loves spicy food? And keeps a lasso in her bag?'

Suddenly, Kerry leaped up and stood on her pillows.

'*What* is that?' she gasped, pointing at the floor. 'Is it a kangaroo?'

The wallaby had lolloped into the room.

'It's a wallaby,' said Harry. 'And it's a she.
Male wallabies don't have pouches. Probably
about three months old, I'd say, judging by
her paw size. That reminds me. Have you got
a bag I can keep her in?'

'Back of the door,' Kerry said, not taking

her eyes off the wallaby.

Harry selected a simple cloth bag, plopped the wallaby in and looped the handles around his neck. Instantly, the wallaby curled up and settled.

'Can I have a biscuit? I'm starving,' he asked.

Kerry handed him the packet and Harry stuffed two into his mouth, munched them quickly and then rushed back to the top of the stairs.

'Wait, Harry,' said Kerry, running after him. 'Why have you got a wallaby? What's going on?'

'I'll explain later,' said Harry. 'Gotta run.

Time's ticking. I must get Mini to the awards. Do me a favour, will you? Check Mum's still outside.'

Kerry ran downstairs and spotted Mum, still battling the goats in the garden. 'All clear,' she called up.

Harry bounded down the stairs.

'Please don't tell Mum anything about this,' he said. 'Definitely don't tell her that I lost Mini. Promise?'

Kerry nodded.

'Headbutt promise?' Harry said.

Harry and Kerry had invented the headbutt promise for serious, important situations just like this. It was the strongest kind of promise of all.

Kerry stood on her tiptoes and gently butted her forehead against Harry's.

'Thanks, sis,' he said, and then zoomed out of the door.

CHAPTER FOURTEEN

Back at the leisure centre, Harry jumped the turnstile again, so quickly that Beverly didn't even notice, and sprinted downstairs to return the flip-flops to their place under the bench outside the changing rooms. He checked the time, 1.55 p.m. – still five minutes until Mini finished her lifeguard shift. Yes!

Harry trotted back upstairs to the pool observation area. He was feeling excited. Finally, after hours of chasing her around, Mini would be with him again. Harry would take her to the hairdresser's appointment, they would get a late lunch, pick a new outfit and then off to the awards. His mum would see how responsible he was – responsible enough to take care of his granny, and definitely responsible enough to have a dog. It was going to be a very happy ending, a spectacular victory, a total and utter triumph, and just, you know, really, really great too.

Harry approached the window that overlooked the pool and stared down.

He heard a noise that sounded like someone
whimpering.

Then he realised that noise was coming
from him.

The pool was empty and so was the
lifeguard chair.

'No!' he cried.

He dashed back to Beverly.

'Where is the lifeguard? What happened
to the pool? It's empty! Sorry – what? How?
Please?'

'Calm down, it's nothing to worry about,'
said Beverly. 'One of our older customers
lost his false teeth. They floated out and
have blocked the filter. The pool's closed

while they fish them out.'

'What about the lifeguard? The little woman with white hair?'

'Why do you want to know?' asked Beverly. 'Are you her son?'

'No, I'm her grandson. I'm eleven. I was dressed as a chipmunk earlier on, only you thought I was a hamster, remember? Anyway, do you know where she went?'

Beverly shook her head. Harry let out a squeak of stress (which actually did sound a bit hamster-y), the baby wallaby bouncing against his chest.

He looked left and right for Mini, but she wasn't there.

How could she keep on disappearing?

How had he lost her again?

He should never have taken his eyes off her. He should not have gone home to change. He should have learned from his mistakes.

Harry ran back out on to the street. He cursed inside his head, telling himself he was a 'drubnut' and 'a total clack-biscuit'.

He rubbed his hair with his knuckles and took some deep breaths. He was struggling to think straight. He'd been running around after his granny all day, trying to keep his promise to take care of her, hoping to win those precious fifty puppy points, but his granny clearly had other ideas.

What was she playing at? Why was she so determined not to stick to the schedule? Didn't she know how hard she was making life for Harry? Didn't she understand that Harry's mum would be cross as a goose if he didn't get her to the awards? Harry pictured her in full Pan Woman–Goat Nemesis mode, only this time she was chasing *him* around the garden, banging her wooden spoon. He shuddered.

'I have to find Mini. I must not give up,' he said, and began running towards town.

He hadn't got far when he stopped, suddenly, in his tracks. There, in front of him, was the Rodent Awareness Day stand. He was about to hide or run in the opposite direction – he didn't have time for more dancing and photos – when he remembered that last time he was here, he was hidden inside a chipmunk costume. No one had seen his face. No one knew who he was. It was safe to walk past.

People were clustered around a big display case with a sign saying Mouse Town. Inside, there was a model street, complete with model houses, shops and cars. Scurrying in and out of windows and across the roofs were lots of tiny mice.

Harry couldn't resist a quick look. He liked seeing the mice poking their heads out of bedroom windows, like giant rodent residents of a tiny town. Sometimes he felt like a giant resident of a tiny town himself. Harry the Hulk. Tall for his age. Always mistaken for older than he was. Expected to do jobs and act grown-up, and yet still not trusted enough to have a dog.

'This is so cool,' said a familiar voice.

'Keith!' said Harry. 'What are you doing here?'

'Enjoying Mouse Town, obviously,' said Keith. 'Look, there's one in a car, and look at that one coming out of the library. Excellent!'

'My granny is still missing,' Harry blurted. 'I don't know where to look for her.'

'Was she at the theme park in the end?' Keith asked.

'Yes, but she got away, and went to the leisure centre to work as a lifeguard,' said Harry.

'Nice. Lifeguarding – a very cool job,' said Keith. 'Your gran is amazing.'

'Amazing at disappearing. Where should I look now?' Harry asked.

'Definitely look over here,' said Keith. 'They've got a beaver, called Justin. Beavers are rodents too – did you know that?'

Of course Harry knew that. He knew all about rodents, and marsupials, and every other kind of mammal going. In fact, beavers were one of his favourite animals, along with otters and seals.

'When I said where should I

look now, I meant where should I look now for my gran,' said Harry. 'I'm running out of time. I should be at the hairdresser's with her right now.'

Then Harry had a thought.

'Maybe that's where I should go,' he said.

'Interesting. Go on,' said Keith.

'Well, she hasn't done any of the things she was supposed to do today,' Harry said. 'So, you might think there's no way she'll go to the hairdresser's now.'

'Agreed,' said Keith.

'But she never does what I expect her to do, which is probably why she is at the hairdresser's now,' said Harry. 'She hasn't played by the rules all day, so by doing the thing she's supposed to do, at the time she's supposed to do it, she's also not playing by the rules.'

'Excellent detective work, Harry,' Keith said. 'Meet and Tuveg would be very proud of you.'

'You bet they would!' Harry yelled. He patted Keith on the head three times, and then sprinted away.

CHAPTER FIFTEEN

The Hair Today, Bald Tomorrow salon wasn't too far away. Harry was there in a few minutes. He pushed the door open. Inside, the air felt moist and hairdryer warm. It smelt sweetly of shampoo. As Harry scanned the salon, looking for Mini, one of the hairdressers approached him, smiling.

'Can I help?' she said.

'I'm looking for my granny,' said Harry. 'She had an appointment here, round about now.'

'What's her name?' she asked.

'Mini. She's called Mini,' Harry said.

'Is that her real name?'

'No, it's a nickname, because she's really small.'

Harry suddenly realised he didn't know what his granny's real name was.

'Sorry, she's just, er, Mini,' he mumbled, blushing faintly.

'Don't worry. I can work it out. That must have been Marjory Peach,' said the hairdresser, checking the appointments in a diary. 'Our stylist Krissy did her hair. She had a two p.m. appointment but got here early. You've just missed her. She was sitting over there.'

Harry looked where the woman was pointing. An assistant was sweeping up hundreds of white curls from the floor, but the chair where Mini had sat was empty.

Harry gasped and went pale. He slumped down into one of the hairdressing chairs.

'Are you OK? Here, have some water,' said the hairdresser, passing him a cup. 'Are you her personal assistant or something?'

'Grandson. I'm only eleven. I'm Harry.'

He gulped down his drink and then stared blankly into the mirror in front of him. The hairdresser, standing behind him, began to play with Harry's hair, moving his fringe this way and that.

'What are you doing?' Harry asked.

'Sorry! Habit,' she said, pulling her hands back and clamping them under her arms. 'I just love hair. I'm just a hairy kind of person.'

'Can I speak to whoever cut my gran's hair? Krissy, I think you said it was,' Harry asked. 'Perhaps she'll know something.'

'Good idea,' said the hairdresser. 'She's just popped out for some lunch. She won't be long, though. You can wait here. I could even give you a trim, as you're sitting here, if you like.'

Her fingers fluttered eagerly above Harry's hair again, as though playing a tiny invisible piano.

Harry sighed and nodded yes and that was it – she leaped into action like someone had fired a special hairdressing start gun that only hairdressers can hear. She threw a gown around Harry's shoulders, grabbed some scissors and began snipping quickly. Clumps of Harry's dark hair fell on to his shoulders and landed on the bag containing the wallaby, resting in his lap.

The hairdresser was about halfway through the cut when the salon door opened and Krissy walked in, holding a sandwich. She beckoned her over.

'You cut my gran's hair just now. Tiny woman, about this big,' Harry said to her, holding his hand a Mini-sized amount off the floor. 'Did she say what she was doing afterwards? I really need to find her.'

Krissy shook her head.

'She didn't mention anything in particular. She just said she was going home.'

'Going home … ?' said Harry, and then he shot up out of his chair like a cork out of a champagne bottle.

'That's it,' he shouted. 'Oh, fresh crumpets of joy. That's it!'

Home. Mini was going home, after her haircut. Home, as in Harry's house? No, he realised. She was going back to her home, in the next town. It all made perfect sense.

Mini didn't want to go to the awards – she

had said so this morning – and having seen how energetic and adventurous she was, Harry could finally understand.

She didn't want a Lifetime Achievement Award and she definitely didn't want Mum's version of a nice day out – choosing a new outfit, dressing up to look respectable, being fussed over.

She wanted to ride roller coasters, do some lifeguarding and throw pork pies at security guards! And she had. Mission accomplished. Now, all that was left was to head home and swerve the awards altogether.

'I have to go to the bus station,' Harry said, and he ripped off his gown like a superhero tears off his boring suit to reveal his cool, save-the-world onesie underneath.

'Wait!' the hairdresser shouted. 'I've only cut half your hair!'

Too late. The door to the salon had already slammed shut. Harry was off.

CHAPTER SIXTEEN

Harry ran fast. He had to find Mini. He wanted to see her, explain that he understood everything, tell her that she didn't need to run any more. Besides, he had promised his mum he wouldn't let Mini out of his sight. If he could just find her, he would at least have got that bit right.

He arrived at the main town bus station, out of breath, eyes darting here and there, searching for his granny. He peered into bus windows, checked the waiting room and the line of people queuing for tickets. He stared into the faces of everyone he saw. No Mini.

Harry sat down on a bench to think. The

wallaby poked her head out of the bag and stared at him.

'What am I going to do?' Harry asked her. 'I can't find Mini. She's gone. I've lost her again. Again! I know I can't force her to go to the awards if she doesn't want to, but at least if I could find her, we could go home and face Mum together.'

The wallaby carried on staring at Harry.

'I won't win the fifty puppy points, will I?' he said. 'I suppose I just have to hope that Mum will let me carry on doing jobs, and I can win the points that way.'

Harry felt a tear of disappointment prickle in each eye and he sighed heavily. The puppy he'd thought was almost his, almost within touching distance, if only he'd managed to get his gran to the awards show, now seemed to be running off into the mist of the future, getting further and further away.

The wallaby continued to stare at him with her dark eyes. Then he heard his name.

'Harry?'

Was the wallaby speaking to him?

'Harry?'

She *was* speaking to him. Without moving her lips. Maybe her wallaby brain was communicating with his brain. Or maybe he was going mad. Perhaps this was all a bad dream, and he'd wake up in a minute, eat breakfast and go out for a nice day with Keith, Tom and Jonny.

'Harry?'

There it was again. Then Harry felt a hand on his arm. He tore his gaze away from the wallaby's and looked up. He saw a small woman with white – hang on, not white hair, purple hair.

'Mini?' he said. 'Is that you?'

'Of course it is, dear,' said Mini. 'I had my hair dyed. It's Heavenly Lilac. Don't look so shocked. It's only a rinse, it's not permanent. Fun, though, don't you think? Do you love it?'

Harry's mouth dropped open, but he said nothing.

'Are you all right?' she asked.

Still Harry said nothing.

'Toffee?' said Mini, rummaging in her handbag and offering him one.

Harry looked at the toffee in its shiny gold wrapper and felt a hot flash of anger. Toffees had kicked off this whole disastrous day.

Mini stealing toffees in the supermarket.

Mini escaping on the back of a lorry.

Mini riding crazy roller coasters in the theme park ...

And Harry, always a beat behind, sweating and lying and wearing a chipmunk suit and rushing around.

'You ran off!' he exploded. 'You didn't stay with me. I was trying to look after you, you know!'

He leaped to his feet.

'I was supposed to take care of you and get you to the awards. Mum said. She's giving me lots of puppy points for it, and then I'd be so close to finally getting a puppy, which I really, really want more than anything else in the world.'

Harry was panting now, with tears in his eyes. Mini gazed up at him.

'Look at me, Harry,' she said.

Harry tried to look at his granny, but felt unexpectedly shy. He hardly ever yelled like this, especially not at a grown-up; double especially not at his gran. She reached into her bag again and this time pulled out a tissue.

'I thought you only had crazy stuff in your bag,' Harry murmured, taking it.

'I'm still a granny too though,' said Mini.

Harry blew his nose.

'Sorry for shouting,' he said.

'No, I'm sorry,' Mini said, gripping his hand. 'Really sorry. I didn't guess that you would track me all over town; that you would try so hard to take care of me. I thought I'd have a fun day out, then go home. I didn't think enough about you, and your promise to stick with me today. I am truly, truly sorry.'

Harry felt as if all the fight had evaporated out of him, like steam off a Cup-a-Soup. He thumped back down on to the bench.

'I didn't know Mum had offered you puppy points, either,' said Mini.

'Fifty! Loads! I'd be almost at my target,' said Harry, 'and Mum would finally see that I'm ready for a pet. That's why I didn't give up. That's why I followed you. Now it's all gone wrong.'

'No, it hasn't,' said Mini. 'We'll go to the awards, and you'll win the points.'

'But you don't want to go. You don't want to get a Lifetime Achievement Award or wear a hat,' he said. 'You were about to catch a bus home.'

'Well, yes, but ...' said Mini.

'I bet you flooded the shower deliberately, so Mum would have to stay home and sort it out. Then you could do what you wanted all day and skip the awards,' said Harry. 'You did, didn't you?'

'All right, I admit, I did run the shower when I knew I shouldn't have. I even stuffed some loo roll in the drain to make sure it flooded. I am an expert in loo roll, after all,' said Mini. 'But now I know about the puppy points, I've changed my mind. I'll go to the awards and do right by you, Harry. We have time, don't we?'

Harry checked his watch.

'It's twenty to three,' he said.

'Perfect,' said Mini. 'We can have a late lunch first.'

She stood up, grabbed her big bag and marched off.

'Come on,' she called over her shoulder. 'What are you waiting for – Christmas? Bring your kangaroo with you too.'

CHAPTER SEVENTEEN

Mini and Harry went into a cafe. Mini ordered sandwiches and chips and milkshakes from the waiter, then put the menu down and beamed at Harry.

'It's a wallaby, by the way,' Harry said, pointing at the bag around his neck. 'Just so you know. Not a kangaroo. Her fur has lots of different brown and grey shades in it. Kangaroos tend to be a plain sandy colour.'

'Oh, I see,' said Mini.

'And her legs, obviously, are much shorter than a kangaroo's,' Harry added, holding her up for a second so Mini could see. 'She got into my pouch when I was dressed as a chipmunk at Fun Valley.'

'Bet you never imagined when you got up this morning that you'd be dressing as a chipmunk at a theme park today,' Mini said.

'It wasn't as fun as it sounds,' said Harry. 'It was really hot in that suit. All these little kids kept punching my belly and kicking me up the bum!'

'That must have been awful,' Mini said, trying not to smile.

'Don't laugh,' said Harry. But Mini couldn't hold it in, and Harry found, to his surprise, that he laughed too. The wallaby licked his face, which made him laugh even more.

'What's her name?' Mini asked.

'She doesn't have a name yet,' Harry said.

'I might call her Marjory, after you.'

Mini looked shocked.

'How do you know my name's Marjory?'

'Found out at the hairdresser's,' said Harry. 'It's the first time I've ever heard your real name. I think it's nice.'

'It's not. It gets shortened to Marj, which is like butter, only not as good. By the way, I love your new haircut. Long on one side, short on the other. Very chic!'

Harry had forgotten he'd run out halfway through his trim. He touched his lopsided hair and wondered whether he did actually look chic, whatever that was, but then the food arrived and he tucked in hungrily. He was demolishing the last of his chips when a man came over to their table, smiling at Mini.

'Can't wait to see you at the awards show later. You're such a legend. I can see why you need a manager,' he said, pointing at Harry.

'I'm not her manager, I'm her grandson,' said Harry.

'Sorry, right … Nice haircut, by the way. You must be very proud of your gran – inventor of a totally unique kind of loo roll. She changed the world of toilet tissue forever – and all when she was only twenty-one. Amazing!' said the man.

Harry watched him leave and then leaned over the table towards his gran.

'Is that true?' he asked.

Mini nodded.

'It's all because the loo-roll factory in this town burned down and the entire region completely ran out,' she explained. 'There was no loo roll in the shops anywhere nearby, and this was before the internet, so you couldn't buy it online. Everyone was panicking. People were using the pages of books, grass cuttings, children's socks, even pancakes and pitta bread to wipe their bums. It was a disaster.'

'But you saved the day?' asked Harry.

'Well, yes. I worked out a way to use the leaves of a plant that grows all over the town to make loo roll,' said Mini. 'Problem solved.'

'Lucky Leaf loo roll!' said Harry. 'That was you? Mini, that's amazing. You totally deserve the Lifetime Achievement Award. I can't believe you were going to go home and not collect it.'

'Well, it's only loo roll, after all. We all know where it ends up – down the toilet. Besides, I don't like the idea of looking back. This award is about what I achieved in the past, as if that's me done and finished. But I'm not,' said Mini. 'Your mum doesn't get it. She thinks I'm a frail old lady who needs looking after.'

'Well, she thinks I'm a little kid who can't

take care of a pet, just because of a few mistakes,' said Harry. 'It was ages ago, but she won't forget it.'

'She can't see that you've grown up,' said Mini. 'I can though. You've been a trooper today. I can tell you'll make a brilliant dog owner.'

Harry smiled and gulped down the last of his milkshake.

'I'm so excited to see you get your award,' he said. 'You should be proud of what you did. People love you. Let's celebrate that. Doesn't mean you won't do more amazing stuff in the future. In fact, I know you will.'

Mini smiled at Harry.

'All right, but listen, if we are celebrating my loo-roll achievements, there's one other thing I'd love to do today – visit the loo-roll factory, here in town.'

Harry frowned, thinking about the new outfit and hat he was supposed to get for his granny, and how little time they had until the awards started.

'Forget Mum's schedule,' said Mini, reading his mind. 'Let's do things our way now, the two of us, together. A bit of fun before the awards ceremony. What do you say?'

A bit of fun? Fun? What was fun? Harry's day had been so stressful, he'd almost forgotten that fun was a 'thing'. How did it work, what did it taste like, could you always 'do fun', even if you were out of practice? Was it like riding a bicycle? He wasn't sure, but he had to find out.

'All right then,' said Harry, a smile spreading across his face like a sunrise. 'I'm in. Yes to doing things our way. Yes to fun. Let's do this. Let's visit that loo-roll factory, right now!'

CHAPTER EIGHTEEN

The Sheets Ahead factory wasn't far away. It had grand entrance gates, and two tall chimneys, and inside, forklift trucks whizzed about moving pallets piled high with toilet paper and kitchen roll.

Mini marched inside.

'Two tickets for the tour, please,' she said.

'One child, one senior citizen.'

'He doesn't look like a child,' said the man who worked there, pointing at Harry. 'Is he your carer?'

'I have no need of a carer, thank you very much,' said Mini. 'This is my grandson, Harry Pickles. He's eleven, he just happens to be tall for his age.'

Marjory popped her head out of Harry's bag.

'And before you ask, that is a wallaby, not a kangaroo,' said Mini.

The man frowned a bit but then handed over the tickets. Harry and Mini waited with a group of six other people and then, a moment or two later, Mr Ply, the manager, arrived to start the tour.

'Welcome to the Sheets Ahead factory,' he said. 'Our passion is toilet tissue and kitchen towel. We produce quilted, padded and super-soft varieties. We also do perfumed sheets.'

'How posh!' Mini said.

'Our rolls are premium quality. They have what we call in the industry excellent "finger-breakthrough" resistance,' Mr Ply went on.

Mini giggled. Harry grinned and elbowed her in the ribs.

'We convert four hundred and fifty tonnes of paper per month into disposable household products,' Mr Ply continued. 'We are extremely enthusiastic about toilet tissue and I hope, on this tour, this enthusiasm will rub off on you.'

Mini laughed really loud now.

'Sorry about my gran,' said Harry, smiling and not looking sorry at all. 'She's got no manners.'

Mr Ply frowned and squinted to see who Harry was standing next to, and when he saw Mini, his eyes lit up.

'Oh, my goodness! What an honour,' he said. 'Mini, if I had known you were coming on the tour, I would have ...'

'You would have what?' asked Mini. 'Baked me a cake?'

'Or maybe you could have put some decorations up?' Harry added. 'At least some more bunting.'

'Oh yes, bunting,' said Mini. 'I do love the bunting.'

Mr Ply laughed and blushed.

'Everybody, we are truly privileged to have the inventor of Lucky Leaf loo roll with us today,' said Mr Ply to the rest of the tour group. 'A true pioneer – Mrs Marjory Peach, better known as Mini. We still manufacture Lucky Leaf in the factory. It's a bestseller and here – HERE! – is the woman who invented it!'

The other people looked at Mini and began clapping and cheering. Mini smiled.

'You're very kind,' she said, 'but I simply came up with a new kind of loo roll, so everyone could wipe their bums and get on with their lives. Speaking of which, Mr Ply, can we get on with the tour, please? My grandson and I don't have much time.'

'Absolutely, of course,' said Mr Ply. 'If you'd like to follow me.'

Mr Ply led the group on to the factory floor. It was noisy, with massive machines whirring and humming, and there was a pulpy, papery smell in the air.

'It takes 0.27 seconds to make a roll of toilet tissue,' said Mr Ply.

'Call it loo roll!' Mini said. 'Nobody says

toilet tissue, not in the real world. And speak up, will you, dear? I'm a bit deaf.'

Mr Ply cleared his throat and continued.

'Here at the Sheets Ahead factory, we produce around 4.7 million rolls a day.'

'Bit louder, please!' yelled Mini.

'Once we have squashed and pressed the wood pulp to make paper,' shouted Mr Ply, 'we roll and dry it, and then form it into giant rolls here.'

They walked over to two enormous rolls, which even towered over Harry. They looked like regular loo rolls as seen through a huge magnifying glass.

'These "mother" rolls are waiting to be

unfurled, made into smaller rolls and then cut up with spinning saws. Each one produces ten thousand rolls of household toilet tissue,' Mr Ply explained.

Harry expected Mini to shout out 'loo roll' again, but she didn't. In fact, she was nowhere to be seen. Had she run off again? Then he spotted a pair of size-three sneakers disappearing inside one of the supersized rolls. He peered in, and there was Mini, crawling through the middle.

'That looks awesome!' Harry said, clambering in after his granny.

'Everything all right back there?' asked Mr Ply.

'Everything's fine,' said Mini, appearing head first out of the giant roll, dragging her large handbag after her. 'That was terrific. Super, isn't it, Harry?'

He called out from inside, 'Yes, it's like crawling through a cardboard sausage,' and then started giggling.

'Precisely,' said Mini. 'You should all try it.'

'No, no, don't do that,' said Mr Ply, his hands forming two stop signs. 'Each of those weighs over a tonne. If one rolled free, it could crush you.'

'Death by loo roll,' said Mini, chuckling. 'Do carry on, dear.'

CHAPTER NINETEEN

Mr Ply led the group to another side of the factory.

'Here's where the magic happens,' said Mr Ply. 'This is the slicing machine. That long roll comes along the belt and into the machine, where it is cut up. Now, come round to the other side, and there! See? You can recognise these as loo rolls now.'

Everybody smiled, and one person clapped, as individual loo rolls tumbled out of the slicing machine and on to a conveyor belt that whizzed them away.

Mini and Harry gazed at the rolls rushing past for a while, hypnotised by the blur of white, and then Mr Ply led them outside, where a forklift truck was loading enormous packs of loo roll on to a lorry.

'I've always wanted a ride in one of those,' Harry said, pointing at the forklift.

'Feel free to sit in the cab if you like,' said Mr Ply.

He motioned to the driver, who hopped out

and then Harry climbed in.

'Make some room,' said Mini, squishing in next to him and sitting in the driver's seat.

'This little truck is capable of eight miles per hour,' Mr Ply told the tour group, 'although only with a skilled driver.'

Harry admired all the levers and buttons. He might as well have been sitting in a space rocket, he was that impressed. Then he glanced at his watch.

'Oh peanuts,' he said. 'Mini, we should go. It's almost four o'clock and the Metro Hotel is quite a long walk away.'

'Righto, dear,' said Mini. 'Only, I don't much feel like walking.'

Then Harry spotted it. That twinkle in Mini's eye.

'Mini, are you having ideas again?' Harry asked.

'Mr Ply did say this can go eight miles per hour,' said Mini, 'and we are running a bit late.'

She reached for the key that was still hanging in the ignition.

'And I have always wanted a ride in one of these,' said Harry, a twinkle appearing in his eye now.

Mini turned the key and the forklift truck rumbled into life.

'Oh, I say, Mrs Peach, I wouldn't do that,'

said Mr Ply, rushing forwards.

'Don't worry, dear,' she shouted out of the cab, 'I've been driving forklift trucks all my life.'

Then she pushed her foot down on the accelerator and the truck lurched forwards, sending everyone running for cover.

'Can you really drive this thing?' Harry asked.

'Of course I can,' said Mini, zigzagging crazily towards the gates. 'I'm just a bit rusty.'

'All right then, if you say so,' said Harry, holding on tight. 'Hit it, Mini. Full speed ahead. We've got an awards do to get to.'

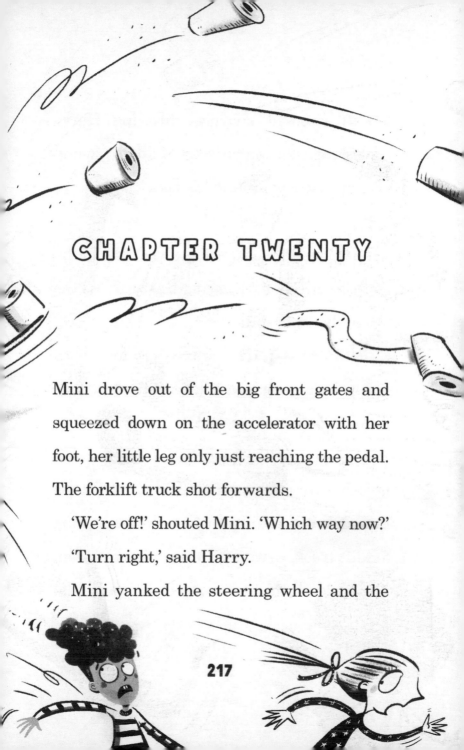

CHAPTER TWENTY

Mini drove out of the big front gates and squeezed down on the accelerator with her foot, her little leg only just reaching the pedal. The forklift truck shot forwards.

'We're off!' shouted Mini. 'Which way now?'

'Turn right,' said Harry.

Mini yanked the steering wheel and the

forklift swerved sharply, throwing Harry across the cab. Marjory the wallaby swung about in the bag around his neck.

'No, sorry, left,' he said.

Mini heaved the steering wheel back in the opposite direction, throwing Harry across the cab in the other direction.

'**Waarrgghh**, crazy granny with purple hair in charge of a forklift alert! Run for your lives,' he shrieked, laughing.

They were on the busy high street now, and quickly attracted attention. Well, of course they did. When did you last see a speeding forklift truck, driven by a tiny senior citizen, racing down the main street of your local town, with a giant child with lopsided hair beside her? Exactly.

Now, though, unlike earlier in the supermarket, Harry found he didn't mind that people were looking at him and Mini. He was happy for people to gawp. He even leaned out of the cab window, waving and shouting, 'Good people of the high street, I love you all!'

When Harry ducked back inside the cab, he checked the time again.

'Amazing, we're actually on time! After everything!' he said. 'This is awesome, Mini. Just keep going. The hotel's not far now.'

Then Harry heard something, faint at first, but getting louder. A siren. He looked behind him. He could see blue lights flashing, some way off. He remembered the telescope in Mini's bag and grabbed it. Squinting through it, he could now clearly see a police car and the police officer driving it. The man was bald, with a rather small head and a red face. He looked, Harry thought, like an angry meatball.

'What's the matter?' Mini asked.

'A police car,' said Harry.

'Chasing us?' Mini asked.

'Maybe,' said Harry. 'We have just stolen a forklift truck ...'

'Borrowed,' said Mini firmly. 'We have borrowed it. Haven't the police got better things to do, anyway? We're not thieves, we're just having a bit of fun. It's not a crime to have a good time.'

Behind them, the police car was getting closer. The police officer leaned out of the window as it sped along, and raised a loud-hailer to his mouth.

'Stop right now,' he shouted. 'I am Inspector Nugget and I command you to **stop**.'

'What did he say?' Mini asked. 'I am quite deaf, remember.'

'He said he's a Nugget and he wants us to stop,' said Harry, 'but we're so nearly there. Does this thing go any faster? Is there a turbo button?'

Mini shook her head.

'What about in your bag, Mini?' Harry said. 'Anything else that could help?'

He peered inside.

'Penknife, no. Gold spray paint, no. What's this?'

Harry held up a tin.

'Pocket Fog,' said Mini. 'I forgot I had that. Wonderful. Open it and throw it towards the police car.'

Harry yanked the ring pull and lobbed the can. It bounced in the road as thick fog billowed out of it, forming a dense white cloud. Harry couldn't see the police car any more, but he could hear Inspector Nugget slamming on the brakes.

'It worked,' said Harry.

'Excellent. He'll be stuck in there for a minute or two, until the fog lifts,' said Mini.

The forklift surged onwards. Up ahead, Harry spotted the Rodent Awareness Day gathering, still in full swing.

'Nothing can stop us now,' Mini shouted. 'Not the police, not ...'

'A BEAVER!' Harry screamed.
'WATCH OUT!'

There was an enormous beaver, sitting right in the middle of the road. Mini slammed on the brakes. Harry covered his eyes. He couldn't watch. They were going to hit the beaver! They were going to hit the beaver! They were going to ...

SCREEEEEECH!

The tyres squealed on the tarmac as Mini swerved the truck sharply to the left. Then ...

CRASH!

Harry opened his eyes. Mini had missed Justin Beaver, but she had driven straight into Mouse Town.

The miniature wooden town now lay on the ground, smashed to pieces. Mice were streaming out of it, scampering all over the pavement and into the crowds.

'We should get out of here,' said Harry.
'Come on, quick, let's make a run for it.'

He jumped out of the cab, Marjory
bouncing about in the bag around his neck,
and helped Mini down. Then, in the confusion
of swarming mice, screaming people and an
escaped beaver, the two of them took off
up the street.

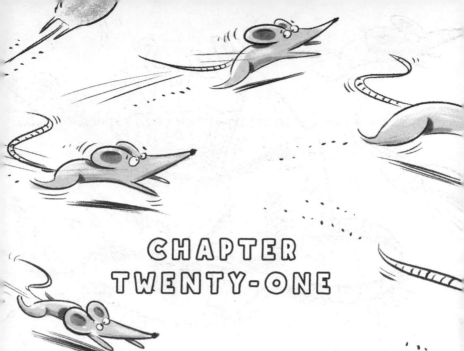

CHAPTER
TWENTY-ONE

Harry and Mini ran towards the Metro Hotel, but they hadn't got far before they heard the siren of Inspector Nugget's police car blaring again.

'Quick, in here,' said Harry, steering Mini into a shop. They huddled by the window and saw the police car whizz past. Using the telescope again, Harry watched it speed off into the distance.

'Inspector Nugget doesn't know where we're heading,' said Harry, 'but he won't give up. He knows what we look like now.'

Then Harry remembered how, when he was dressed as a chipmunk earlier, nobody could tell who he was. He was perfectly hidden behind a costume. Perhaps that was the answer.

'It's not too far to the hotel, but Inspector Nugget could come back at any moment,' said Harry. 'I think, if we're going to make it to the awards safely, we need some kind of disguise.'

'Good idea,' Mini nodded. 'But what?'

Then Harry turned away from the window and, for the first time, realised what kind of shop they had taken cover in. It was a hat shop. Perfect! Mum had insisted that Mini have a new hat today, and now here they were surrounded by them.

'Here for a hat?' asked the shop owner.

'Possibly,' said Harry. 'We're actually on our way to an important awards party at the Metro Hotel. My granny here is winning the Lifetime Achievement Award.'

'How fabulous,' said the shop owner. 'Well, you must have a hat then. How about this? It matches your hair, madam.'

She placed a purple hat with a wide brim and a long orange feather on Mini's head.

'Ooh, it does look rather good,' said Mini, turning this way and that in the mirror. 'The queen would adore it.'

'It's not enough of a disguise though. Quick, Mini, can I have your big red scarf, please?'

She dug it out of her bag and Harry wound it around her little body, covering up her cardie and skirt.

'Do you have any safety pins?' he asked the shop owner.

She nodded, looked a bit confused, but hurried over with them. Harry quickly pinned the scarf here and there, securing it in place. He stood back. Mini gazed at her reflection.

'Oh, it's beautiful. Like a gorgeous red dress,' she said. 'Harry, you're so talented.'

'It's not finished yet,' said Harry.

He took Marjory out of the cloth bag hanging around his neck, and put her down on the shop floor.

'I need the penknife and gold spray paint from your bag,' he said.

Mini passed them to him and Harry quickly cut the handles off the bag, sprayed them gold and tied them around Mini's neck.

'How clever!' she said. 'Looks like a very

expensive necklace, but how will you carry Marjory now?'

Harry had thought of this. He popped her into Mini's giant handbag. She sat neatly on top of all the crazy things Mini kept in there, and her cute little wallaby face just poked out over the side.

'Now, I need to work out a disguise for me too,' said Harry. 'Do you have any loo roll in your bag?'

'Of course,' said Mini, rummaging underneath Marjory until she found some and passed it to Harry.

'Stolen from the Sheets Ahead factory?' he said.

'I see it more as a free gift,' said Mini.

Harry ripped long pieces off the roll and pinned them to his clothes, until he was covered in a shaggy coat of white paper strips.

'How do I look?'

'Spectacular,' said Mini. 'Like a yeti going to a wedding – a sort of dandy yeti.'

Then Harry tried on a top hat. It made him look even taller – amazingly tall, freakishly tall – but he loved it. It was time, he felt, to embrace his height.

'Please, have these hats as my gift,' said the shop owner. 'It's an honour to have a local loo-roll celebrity and her fashion stylist wear them.'

Harry was about to say, 'I'm not her fashion stylist, I'm just her grandson,' but he stopped himself. Why not let the shop owner think that? Hadn't he just designed two new outfits? Yeah, he'd take that.

'Would you like a hat for your pet too?' the shop owner asked. 'I have a range for dogs, which would probably work perfectly on a kangaroo.'

'Wallaby,' Harry said.

The shop owner popped a tiny green hat shaped like a cupcake on Marjory's head, and secured it under her chin with a red ribbon. She looked impossibly cute. Harry and Mini smiled at her and then turned to admire themselves in the mirror.

'I think we look splendid, all three of us,'
said Mini.

'Fully disguised and fully awesome,' said Harry. 'So, are you ready, Mini? I think it's time. Your spotlight moment awaits. Shall we do this?'

Mini nodded and looped her arm through Harry's. The shop owner held the door open and, smiling, they walked out on to the street.

CHAPTER TWENTY-TWO

Harry felt proud and confident walking Mini up the road. She wasn't surging off ahead or disappearing on the back of a lorry. She was right by his side, looking perfect in her red dress, her new purple hat sitting on top of her new purple hair. And there was Marjory the wallaby too, peeping out of her bag, wearing her cute-as-bunnies green hat.

Harry towered above them. For once, though, he didn't feel awkward about his height. He didn't have to explain that he was only eleven. He wasn't trying to blend in. He walked tall, his shaggy loo-roll outfit rustling in the breeze, his top hat soaring towards the skies.

Harry checked his watch as they got close to the Metro Hotel – 4.30 p.m. exactly. Yes! Then he noticed some familiar faces amongst the crowd – Mr Ply from the loo-roll factory, fans from the supermarket, the man who'd chatted with them in the cafe – and spotted the same newspaper photographer who had taken pictures of him at Rodent Awareness Day. He was now snapping the guests as they arrived. Then he noticed a slightly scruffy kid on a bike, watching it all.

'Keith, over here,' Harry shouted.

'Wow! Harry! Awesome outfit. I didn't recognise you,' said Keith, pedalling over. 'This must be your granny. Cool. Pleased to meet you. So glad you found each other. Just like I found my bike, after you dumped it near the clock tower.'

'Sorry about that,' said Harry. 'It's been a busy day.'

'No worries,' said Keith. 'There is a little homemade tracking device in the saddle –

one of my inventions – so it was easy to find. I've also fitted it with a new, super-loud horn.'

He pointed at a big trumpet-shaped instrument on the handlebars.

'It's called **Keith's Considerable Klaxon**.'

'Give it a blast, then,' said Harry, 'and let's get this party started.'

Keith turned a small handle for a few seconds and then pressed a red button on the top of the klaxon. A huge, shrill sound burst out of it. Wow, was it loud! Even slightly deaf Mini had to cover her ears. All the guests jumped and shrieked in shock,

but when they turned and saw Mini
and Harry, a great cheer went up.

Keith now cycled ahead, sounding his klaxon a few more times, parting the crowd so that Mini and Harry could walk up to the front steps of the Metro Hotel. Here, Mini turned and waved to all her fans and admirers.

'Coming in?' Harry asked Keith.

'I'd love to, but I'm halfway through carving a pat of butter. It's going to look like the Eiffel Tower, eventually. I just need to get the legs right. But hey, have a great time,' he said.

Keith cycled away, blasting his klaxon as he went, and Harry pushed open the hotel's doors. Inside, there were sparkling chandeliers and tinkling piano music, and lots more guests too. When they saw Mini they rushed over, passing her packets of Lucky Leaf loo roll to sign, and hugging and kissing her.

Eventually, Harry helped Mini through the crowds to the banqueting suite. It was a giant room, with a stage at one end and a sparkly gold sign saying **CAUGHT SHORT AWARDS** hanging over it. The awards were lined up on one side, each shaped like a golden, shining loo roll.

Harry and Mini sat down at their table, right by the stage, took their hats off, and Harry fed Marjory some petals from the flower arrangement in the middle while they waited for all the other guests to take their seats. Next, waiters brought out trays of delicious food – tiny quiches and mini bowls of soup, miniature sausages in dinky little buns, all kinds of food on sticks, all totally delicious.

Then the lights dimmed, the guests fell silent and a voice boomed out over the speaker system.

'Ladies and gentlemen,' it roared. 'A very warm and friendly loo-roll welcome to the sixteenth annual Caught Short Awards!'

CHAPTER TWENTY-THREE

There were a lot of awards. Who knew loo

roll could be such a rich and diverse world?

There was:

- The Luxury Loo Roll Award
- The Best Foreign Loo Roll Award
- The Rising Star of the
  Loo Roll World Award

- The Most Ingenious Use of Loo Roll in a Domestic Setting Award (the winner had made a glockenspiel out of loo roll)

There were awards for best texture, best illustrations (yes, some loo rolls had pictures on, Harry discovered), best perfume and best specialised loo roll, which was won by loo roll designed for left-handed people.

Harry was amazed, while Mini continued to snigger, just as she had in the loo-roll factory. She laughed particularly loud when the compère, Mr Wad, introduced the Loo Roll Innovation Award. It went to a woman who had created glow-in-the-dark loo roll, so you don't have to turn the light on at night when you go for a wee.

With each award, the winner rushed on to the stage, while the crowd cheered. Some winners started crying, others waved their golden loo-roll trophy above their heads. Each one made a speech, thanking all kinds of people – their window cleaner, Auntie Beryl, that teacher in primary school who believed in them, their gerbil, the Danish royal family, the local male voice choir – but every winner mentioned Mini, and how her designing a completely new loo roll when she was only twenty-one had made them think, I could do that.

'You have inspired so many people, Mini,' Harry said.

Mini raised her eyebrows, in a kind of 'who knew?' way, but she didn't snigger, or say something like 'It's only loo roll for wiping your bum on' this time. Instead, she squeezed Harry's hand affectionately.

Then the lights dipped dramatically, and the banqueting suite fell silent again. A single spotlight shone on Mr Wad.

'And now for the last and most special award of the evening,' he said. 'The award you've all been waiting for. The award that means so very much ... the Lifetime Achievement Award.'

A huge cheer went up.

'The winner is someone you all know and love,' Mr Wad continued. 'A legend of the loo-roll world, who invented an entirely new form of loo roll that we are still enjoying today. But Lucky Leaf loo roll had nothing to do with luck, and everything to do with the personality and drive of our winner. She is inventive, innovative, energetic and truly inspiring. Please welcome to the stage the one, the only ... **Mini!**'

The entire audience shot to its feet, cheering and waving. Harry leaped up too, roaring and whooping. Then he glanced at Mini. Was she blushing? Hang on, was that a tear in her eye?

Mini stood up slowly, and made her way on to the stage. Mr Wad passed her the giant golden award and Mini gazed at it for a second. Then she took the microphone. Everyone went quiet, waiting for her to speak.

'Thank you,' she said.

'We love you, Mini!' someone shouted at the back.

Laughter.

'I love you too,' said Mini, blowing a kiss into the audience. 'Gosh. Well, I suppose you want a speech, do you?'

'Yes, speech!' people shouted.

'I don't actually have a speech prepared,' she continued. 'In fact, I have to admit, I wasn't going to come today.'

The guests all gasped.

'I was being awkward,' Mini said. 'In fact, it was my grandson who persuaded me to come and celebrate with you all and I'm very pleased that he did. It's been really, really lovely to see so many old friends.'

There was more cheering.

'Now, if I could just invite my grandson up

on to the stage,' she said, beckoning to Harry.

He hopped up, with Marjory in his arms. His loo-roll outfit rustled and the stage lights picked out his lopsided haircut perfectly.

'Nice wallaby,' someone at the back shouted.

'Thank you,' said Harry. Finally, someone realised she wasn't a kangaroo ...

'Harry deserves a very special mention,' said Mini. 'He never gave up on his promise to get me here today, in one piece and on time. He designed my beautiful outfit. Most of all, he made me see sense. So, Harry, this award is for both of us. For the things I've achieved in the past, and for all the things you and I will go on to achieve in the years to come.'

Then Mini folded Harry into a hug, smothering Marjory in her warm cuddle too.

'Thank you for everything,' Mini whispered. 'You're the best grandson ever.'

Harry felt relief and happiness trickle over him, like toffee sauce over a blob of ice cream. He closed his eyes, all the mad moments from his crazy day flashing through his mind, like a demented home movie, while the audience cheered and clapped for what seemed like forever until, out of nowhere, a sound ripped through the room.

'Hands in the air, you two. You're under arrest.'

CHAPTER TWENTY-FOUR

Inspector Nugget was standing at the back of the banqueting suite, his loudhailer pressed to his mouth.

'Finally tracked you down,' he said. 'Now, hands in the air.'

Mini put her award down and Harry put Marjory down and they raised their hands slowly as Inspector Nugget made his way past the tables of shocked guests and climbed on to the stage.

'I'm arresting you, Harry Pickles, for theft of a costume from Fun Valley Adventure Resort,' said Inspector Nugget. 'And I'm arresting you, Marjory Peach, also known as Mini, for theft of a forklift truck.'

'You can put the loudhailer down,' said Mini. 'We're standing right in front of you.'

Inspector Nugget lowered it. His meatball face looked rather small and naked now, more of a meatball bearing.

'You can't arrest my grandson, though,' said Mini. 'He's a minor.'

'A coal miner?' said the inspector.

'No, a child,' said Mini. 'He's only eleven.'

'Really? He's massive,' said the inspector. 'He looks like he's eighteen. Oh well, I can at least arrest you.'

'Actually, I've got the forklift truck back now, so let's just say Mini borrowed it,' said a voice.

It was Mr Ply, from the Sheets Ahead factory. He pushed his way to the front.

'Mini, you must be an excellent forklift driver,' he said. 'Not a scratch on it, even after crashing into Mouse Town. You can have a job driving trucks in my factory any time.'

'Oh, I'd enjoy that,' said Mini.

'We're also developing a new hyper-soft eco-tissue, made from potato peelings and used teabags. We could do with your expertise, if you'd like to get involved,' he said.

'I'd absolutely love to,' said Mini. 'No need to pay me, though, it would be my pleasure.'

'We could pay you in loo roll,' said Mr Ply. 'How does a lifetime supply sound?'

The crowd cheered.

'Quiet!' Inspector Nugget barked. **'Enough!** I am trying to fight crime here.

Harry, I can still caution you for stealing a costume from Fun Valley.'

Someone else pushed to the front now. It was Liz, the props manager from the theme park.

'There's no need to do that, Inspector,' Liz said. 'We can easily spare a chipmunk costume. In fact, Harry, looking at your outfit here, you're obviously a very talented designer. Would you be interested in working on some new costumes for Fun Valley?'

'Yes, please,' Harry said. 'I've got loads and loads of ideas for how to make them less hot and easier to get on and off.'

'Great,' said Liz. 'Come back to the theme

park tomorrow and we can talk about it. I can also arrange free rides for you and Mini, and your friends, if you like.'

Harry's eyes lit up. He could take Keith, Tom and Jonny. The four of them would get their fun day together, after all. He couldn't wait to tell them.

'What about Marjory?' he asked.

'Bring her back tomorrow too,' said Liz. 'She looks very happy with you right now.'

'Ah yes, theft of that kangaroo,' barked Inspector Nugget. 'I can definitely caution you for that.'

'She's a wallaby, Inspector,' Harry said.

'Don't you lecture me on wildlife, sonny,'

said Inspector Nugget. 'I don't care whether that creature is a kangaroo, a wallaby or Puff the Magic Dragon, she's not yours.'

'I didn't steal her, though,' said Harry. 'She got into my costume. She hid in the chipmunk pouch.'

'Chipmunks don't have pouches,' someone called out.

'Silence,' Inspector Nugget snapped back.

'So, in fact, she stowed away,' said Harry. 'You could charge her for that if you want.'

'Yes, arrest the wallaby!' somebody in the crowd shouted, and then everyone laughed and began chanting:

'Arrest the wallaby!

'Arrest the wallaby! 'Arrest the wallaby!'

Inspector Nugget looked confused. He raised the loudhailer to his mouth again, then changed his mind and just stood there for a while looking very cross and disappointed. Finally, the chanting and laughter died down.

'All right, you two, it seems I can't arrest you or charge you or any of that, but I would ask you to behave in a more appropriate manner in future,' he said. 'All right?' And then he climbed off the stage.

'Not much chance of that happening,' said Mini. 'Now he's out of the way, all that remains to do is to turn up the music, as loud as you can. I feel like **dancing**.'

Mr Wad cranked up the music and Mini and Harry began bobbing up and down as a shower of golden glitter rained on them from above. All the other guests joined in, hopping on to the stage, whooping and laughing and letting off party poppers.

Mr Ply did some breakdancing and in between dancing, Mini chatted to her friends and introduced them all to Harry, and the

two of them were hugged and kissed by everyone. The party partied on for a good long while, until later, much later, Mini climbed down off the stage and slumped into her chair.

Harry sat down next to her.

'Are you tired, Mini?' he asked.

'I'm never tired,' said Mini.

'No, of course you're not. That's cool. The thing is, I am a bit tired. Perhaps we should go. Mum will want to hear about the day, after all,' said Harry.

Mini raised her eyebrows.

'Well, maybe we won't tell her *all* about the day,' Harry said.

They both chuckled quietly for a moment and then stood up and said their goodbyes to the other guests. Then Mr Wad began singing

'For She's a Jolly Good Loo Roll', the song sung at the end of every Caught Short Awards, and all the guests joined in as Mini and Harry waved and walked away.

CHAPTER
TWENTY-FIVE

'We're home,' Harry called as he opened the front door.

'In the sitting room,' Mum called back. 'Can't wait to hear all about ... Oh! What on earth are you wearing, Harry?'

'Is that loo roll?' Kerry asked.

'Sure is, sis,' said Harry. 'Thought it was a

good look for the Caught Short Awards.'

'Harry made both our outfits,' Mini said. 'He's so clever.'

'And we went to the hairdresser's, as you can see by Mini's lovely purple hair – it's Heavenly Lilac,' Harry said. 'I had a bit of a trim too.'

He took off his top hat to reveal his lopsided haircut.

'And just look at my award. Isn't it gorgeous?' said Mini. 'Feel it – it's really heavy.'

Mini passed the massive award to Mum, who stared at it suspiciously, like she expected it to squirt water at her, or bits to fall off it, like a clown car.

'I did everything you asked me to do,' said Harry. 'Hairdresser's, a new outfit and even a hat, then I took Mini to the awards, which was totally awesome, and brought her home again, safe as bricks. So, that means I've won my fifty puppy points, haven't I?'

'Not. So. Fast,' said Mum firmly. 'A police officer came round this afternoon. He said something about you stealing a truck, Mini?'

'How weird,' said Mini. 'I don't know anything about police or trucks or stolen anything, do you, Harry?'

'Nothing at all,' said Harry. 'He must have

got the wrong address. Now, how about a nice cup of tea?'

'Good idea,' said Mini, and the two of them marched into the now completely dry kitchen, followed by Mum and Kerry. Mini plonked her handbag down on the table and Marjory the wallaby poked her head out.

'Why is there a kangaroo in your bag?' Mum asked.

'She's a wallaby,' said Mini, Harry and Kerry at exactly the same time, then the three of them burst out laughing.

'I don't understand,' said Mum.

'Did you get the shower fixed?' Mini asked.

'Hope so. I might be coming to stay a bit more

often, now that I've got a new job at the loo-roll factory. Harry's going to be designing costumes at Fun Valley too.'

'I still don't understand,' said Mum.

'That's all right, dear,' said Mini. 'The only thing you need to understand is that Harry is a truly special young man. He took care of me and young Marjory here, all day, through thick and thin, ups and downs.'

Mum's eyes narrowed.

'What ups and downs?' she asked. 'Is there something you're not telling me? Have you been having ideas? You seem a bit weird, both of you. You've got twinkles in your eyes. I don't like it.'

'Relax, Mum, everything's fine,' said
Harry.

'Yes, and I'd say Harry's definitely won his
fifty points,' Kerry said, standing by the
puppy points chart, holding a marker pen.
'Look, Harry, I'm going to add
them on.'

Kerry wrote the new total:
475.

'Only twenty-five points to go and I get a dog,' Harry said. 'This. Is. Brilliant.'

Then a bleating sound came from the garden. It was Primrose and Daisy, scampering towards the rose bushes.

'Not again!' Mum shrieked. 'The goats! They got in at lunchtime – I've no idea how – and now they're back. I can't stand it! Pass me that pan and wooden spoon.'

But before she could transform into Pan Woman–Goat Nemesis, Harry stood up.

'Wait,' he said. 'There may be another way.'

CHAPTER
TWENTY-SIX

Harry pointed at Mini's huge handbag.

'May I use that weird flute you've got in your bag?' he asked.

'Oh, you mean the pungi?' said Mini. 'It's very hard to play, Harry, and I'm not sure it works on goats, only snakes.'

'I'd like to try,' said Harry.

He found the pungi in the bag – it looked like a wooden recorder with a bulge at one end – then put his top hat on and strode out into the garden. Mum, Mini and Kerry watched him through the window.

'What is he doing?' Mum asked.

Harry was performing a little dance, waving his hands about in front of the goats' faces, the loo-roll strips rippling around him like a wheat field in the wind. Then he raised the pungi to his mouth and began to play it. It sounded terrible, like someone stamping on bagpipes, but the goats stared up at Harry, as if they were listening intently. Then he ushered them towards the fence and, quickly

and quietly, they walked back through the
hole and into their own garden.

'Astonishing,' gasped Mum. 'Completely
astonishing. Harry made them go back next
door. No pans, no wooden spoons.'

'Nice work,' agreed Kerry.

Harry returned to the kitchen and Mum hugged him hard.

'What's that for?' he asked, surprised.

'You charmed the goats. You controlled them completely, with that musical instrument thing. Why have you never done that before?'

'I didn't have the pungi before,' said Harry. 'Plus, I don't know, I just feel different today. I feel like I could do anything.'

'Incredible,' said Mum.

'Incredible enough to give me the final twenty-five points?' asked Harry, quick as a flash.

Mum's eyebrows shot up.

'What's this? Negotiating? It's not like you to be so pushy, Harry,' said Mum.

'Like I say, I feel different today.'

'Go on, give him the points,' said Kerry.

'He definitely deserves them,' said Mini.

'Shush, you two,' Mum snapped. 'Let me think about it.'

The thinking went on for what felt like ages. Harry studied his mum's face, but couldn't guess what she would decide. Then, finally, Mum looked at Harry sternly.

'Right. I'm impressed by how you charmed the goats, Harry, and if you can control a puppy like you controlled Primrose and Daisy, you are probably ready.'

'Ready? What does that mean?' Harry asked. 'Ready for a puppy? Is that a yes? Is it? Is it?'

'It's a yes,' said Mum.

Harry shot into the air, like he'd been fired from a rocket, and almost banged his head on the ceiling.

'**A-MAZ-ING!!**' he roared, stretching out each syllable.

'But only – **ONLY** – if you keep the goats out too,' Mum said.

'I will, of course, I promise,' Harry panted. 'Oh wow, wow, wow! I've done it! I've got five hundred puppy points. I am actually getting a dog!'

Then he picked his mum up and bounced her around in his arms, while she shrieked but also laughed. When he finally put her down, she straightened her hair and muttered something about needing a lie-down on the sofa.

Once Mum had left the kitchen, Kerry slapped Harry hard on the back.

'Amazing job, bro!' she said.

'Yes, congratulations, Harry,' said Mini. 'I'm so proud of you.'

'Harry the Hulk – large and in charge,' said Harry, beating his chest with his fists.

'I knew you were talented, but even so, I am amazed you managed to charm the goats with that pungi,' said Mini.

'Nothing to be amazed about, Mini,' said Harry, a twinkle twinkling in his eye once more. 'I've just got a way with animals. What can I say? It's a gift, I suppose.'

'Wait, you've got that super-cheeky look on your face,' said Kerry, poking him in the ribs. 'I haven't seen that since you were eight. What's going on?'

'Nothing!' Harry protested, squirming and trying not to laugh. 'I don't know what you're on about. I charmed the goats, just as Mum said. End of story.'

Kerry jabbed him a few more times, extra hard.

'All right, all right,' Harry shouted, holding his hands up in submission. 'I admit those toffees I gave the goats might have had something to do with it.'

'Toffees?' Kerry said.

'Yeah, toffees. I slipped them a few before I did my magic dance. They were so busy chewing them, they hardly noticed being herded back through the fence. I guess it was handy, in the end, that you "borrowed" them from the supermarket, Gran. I always suspected those goats had a sweet tooth.'

'So, toffees kicked off our adventures today, and now they've finished them too,' Mini said. 'It's a happy ending.'

'Well, it will be once I finally make it to the toilet,' said Harry, dashing for the door. 'I've been dying to go all day.'

'Need this?' Mini asked, plucking a loo roll from her handbag and holding it out towards Harry.

He pointed at the sheets on his costume and grinned.

'That's all right, Gran,' he said. 'I think I've got loo roll covered. Or you could say it's got me covered. Now, if you'll excuse me. Nature calls!'

CAN HARRY FIND

HIS GRANNY???

BORED WITH YOUR BROTHER?

SICK OF YOUR SISTER?

READY FOR A BRAND-NEW, SUPERCOOL SIBLING?

READ ON FOR AN EXTRACT FROM THIS LAUGH-OUT-LOUD ADVENTURE FROM

Jo SIMMONS

CHAPTER ONE

CLICK!

CHANGE BROTHERS AND SWITCH SISTERS TODAY WITH

www.siblingswap.com

The advert popped up in the corner of the screen. Jonny clicked on it instantly. The Sibling Swap website pinged open, showing smiling brothers and happy sisters, all playing and laughing and having a great time together.

What crazy alternative universe was this? Where were the big brothers teasing their little brothers about being rubbish at climbing and slow at everything? Where were the wedgies and ear flicks? What about the name-calling? This looked like a world

Jonny had never experienced, a world in which brothers and sisters actually *liked* each other!

'Oh sweet mangoes of heaven!' Jonny muttered.

It was pretty bonkers, but it was definitely tempting. No, scrap that: it was *essential*. Jonny couldn't believe his luck. Just think what Sibling Swap could offer him.

A new brother. A *better* brother. A brother who didn't put salt in his orange squash, who didn't call him a human sloth, who didn't burp in his ear. That kind of brother.

Jonny had to try it. He could always return the new brother if things didn't work out. It was a no-brainer.

He clicked on the application form.

What could go wrong?

CHAPTER TWO

FIGHT, FATE, FORMS

Only a little while before Jonny saw the Sibling Swap advert, he and his older brother, Ted, had had a fight. Another fight.

It was a particularly stupid fight, and it had started like all stupid fights do – over something stupid. This time, pants. But not just any pants. The Hanging Pants of Doom.

Jonny and Ted were walking their dog, Widget, on the nearby Common. They arrived at a patch of woodland, where an exceptionally large and colourful pair of men's pants had been hanging in a tree for ages. These pants had become legendary over the years the brothers had been playing here. There was a horrible glamour about them. The boys were grossed out and slightly scared of them, but could never quite ignore them. And so the pants had become the Hanging Pants of Doom, and now, unfortunately, Jonny had just lobbed Widget's Frisbee into the tree. It was stuck in a branch, just below the mythical underwear.

'Oh swear word,' said Jonny.

'Nice one!' said Ted. 'You threw it up there, so you have to get it down.'

Jonny frowned. Two problems presented themselves. One was the fact that the Frisbee was very close to the pants, making the possibility of touching the revolting garment very real. Second, Jonny wasn't very good at climbing.

'Go on, Jonny, up you go,' teased Ted. 'Widget can't wait all day for his Frisbee. Climb up and get it ... What's that? You're rubbish at climbing? Sorry, what? You would prefer it if I went and got the Frisbee, as I'm truly excellent at climbing?'

'All RIGHT!' fumed Jonny, ripping off his jacket. 'I'll climb up and get it. Look after my coat.'

'Thanks!' said Ted. 'I might use it as a blanket. You're so slow, we could be here until midnight.'

Jonny began his climb slowly, as Ted had predicted, and rather shakily, as Ted had also predicted.

'I'm just taking my time, going carefully. Don't rush me!' said Jonny, as he reached for the next branch.

'Spare us the running commentary,' Ted said.

After several minutes, a tiny dog appeared below the tree, followed by its elderly owner, and it began yapping up at Jonny.

'That's my brother up there,' Ted said to the

lady, pointing up. 'He's thrown his pants into the tree again and has to go and get them.'

The lady squinted up. Her dog continued yip-yapping.

'Oh yes, I see,' she said. 'Well, they're rather splendid pants, aren't they? I can see why he wants to get them back. Are those spaceships on them?'

'Cars,' said Ted.

'Very fetching,' said the lady. 'But he shouldn't throw them into the trees again. A magpie might get them.'

'That's what I told him,' said Ted, trying not to laugh. 'Sorry, I better go and help or we'll be here until Christmas. He's like a human sloth!'

With that, Ted bounced up into the tree, pulling himself quickly up its branches and passing his brother, just as Jonny was within touching distance of the Frisbee.

'Got it!' said Ted, snatching the Frisbee and tossing it down to Widget, before swinging off a branch and landing neatly on his feet. 'You can come down now, bro. Unless you really do want to touch the Pants of Doom. You're pretty close, actually. Look! They're just there.'

Jonny made a noise in his throat – a bit like a growl – and felt his face burning bright red. He was shaking with anger and humiliation as he slowly began making his way down.

By the time the brothers banged back into the house, Jonny was speechless with fury. He ran upstairs. He could hear his mum telling him off for slamming the front door, but too bad. He smashed his bedroom door shut too. There! How's that? He was sick of Ted teasing him, sick of being the younger brother. And as for telling that old lady that the Hanging Pants of Doom were *his* ...

Jonny flipped open his laptop and, miraculously, there was the Sibling Swap website telling him that all this could change. What perfect timing. Had the Sibling Swap team climbed into his head and read his thoughts? Who cared?

He read the home page:

SOMETIMES YOU DON'T GET THE BROTHER OR SISTER YOU DESERVE, BUT HERE AT SIBLING SWAP, WE AIM TO PUT THAT RIGHT. WITH SO MANY BROTHERS AND SISTERS OUT THERE, WE CAN MATCH YOU TO THE PERFECT ONE!

His heart began to beat faster.

SWAPPING YOUR BROTHER OR SISTER HAS NEVER BEEN EASIER WITH SIBLING SWAP! SIMPLY FILL OUT THE APPLICATION FORM

AND WE WILL SUPPLY YOU WITH A NEW BROTHER OR SISTER WITHIN TWENTY-FOUR HOURS, CAREFULLY CHOSEN FROM OUR MASSIVE DATABASE OF POSSIBLE MATCHES. OUR DEDICATED TEAM OF SWAP OPERATIVES WORKS 24/7 TO FIND THE BEST MATCH FOR YOU, BUT IF YOU ARE NOT COMPLETELY HAPPY, YOU CAN RETURN YOUR REPLACEMENT SIBLING FOR A NEW MATCH OR YOUR ORIGINAL BROTHER OR SISTER.

Amazing! For the first time in his almost ten years, this website was offering Jonny power, choice, freedom! It felt good! He rubbed his hands together and began filling out the form.

First, there were two options:

ARE YOU SWAPPING A SIBLING?

ARE YOU PUTTING YOURSELF UP TO BE SWAPPED?

'Easy,' Jonny muttered. 'I'm the one doing the swapping. Me. I have the power!' He did a sort of evil genius laugh as he clicked on the top box. By Tic Tacs, this was exciting! Next, the form asked:

ARE YOU SWAPPING A BROTHER OR SISTER?

'Also easy,' muttered Jonny. 'Brother.'

Then:

WOULD YOU LIKE TO RECEIVE A BROTHER OR A SISTER?

Jonny clicked the box marked 'Brother'. Then he had to add some information about himself.

AGE: NINE.

HOBBIES: BIKING, SWIMMING, COMPUTER GAMES, DOUGHNUTS, MESSING ABOUT.

LEAST FAVOURITE THINGS:

• **MY BROTHER, TED (HE TEASES ME ALL**

THE TIME AND RECKONS HE'S COOL JUST BECAUSE HE GOES TO SECONDARY SCHOOL)
- **BEING NINE (I *AM* NEARLY TEN, BUT CAN I HAVE A BROTHER WHO IS YOUNGER THAN ME OR MAYBE THE SAME AGE PLEASE?)**
- **SPROUTS**
- **CLIMBING**
- **BEING SICK**

Then there was a whole page about the kind of brother Jonny might like. He quickly ticked the following boxes: fun; adventurous; enjoys food; enjoys sports and swimming; likes dogs. He didn't tick the box marked 'living' or the one marked 'human'. He just wanted a brother, so it was obvious, wasn't it?

That ought to do it, Jonny reckoned. His heart was galloping now. In just three minutes it was ready to send. He sat back in his chair. 'Just one click,' he said, 'and I get a brother upgrade by this time tomorrow. Friday, in fact! Ready for the weekend!'

Jonny felt slightly dizzy. He giggled quietly to himself. He felt giddy with power! All he had to do was send off the form. Easy! But then he hesitated … Should he do this? Was it OK? Would he get into trouble? Jonny's dad no longer lived with him and Ted, so he might not notice, but what would his mum say? She'd be pleased, Jonny decided quickly. Yes! After all, she was fed up with Jonny and Ted arguing. This was the perfect solution. Then, with a tiny frown, he wondered how Ted might feel about being swapped, but before he could puzzle this out, there was his brother again, shouting up the stairs.

'Dinner, loser!' Ted yelled. 'Let me know if you need help climbing down the stairs.

They *are* quite steep. It could take you a while.'

That was it! For the second time that day, Jonny felt the anger bubbling up inside like a can of shaken Pixie Fizz. Enough! Double enough!

'So I'm the rubbish younger brother, am I? Well, here's one thing I can do really brilliantly,' he muttered and, jutting out his chin, hit the send button.

CLICK!

'Done!' he said, and slammed the laptop shut.

HEAD TO
www.siblingswap.com
TODAY

... your future
sibling awaits!

Change brothers and switch sisters!

Sometimes you don't get the brother or sister you deserve,
but here at Sibling Swap, we aim to put that right.
With so many brothers and sisters out there,
we can match you to the perfect one!

So what are you waiting for?
Get SWAPPING!

- Take the quiz to find your perfect brother or sister
- Meet the founder of Sibling Swap
- Download fun activities and games to play with
  (or without) your sibling!

KEITH WANTS TO WIN THE
JUNIOR MEGA BRAIN QUIZ.

THE PROBLEM IS — HE'S NOT REALLY
A GENIUS. EVEN WORSE, HIS SISTER
ACTUALLY *IS*, AND KEITH WILL HAVE TO
GO HEAD-TO-HEAD AGAINST HER.
KEITH NEEDS TO GET SUPER SMART,
AND FAST!

COULD HE JUST STEAL HIS SISTER'S BRAIN?

LOOK OUT FOR THIS
LAUGH-OUT-LOUD ADVENTURE FROM

JO SIMMONS

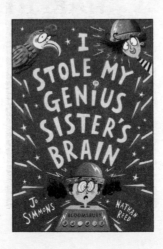

TOM CAN'T WAIT FOR HIS
LUCKY BIRTHDAY. IT'S AN EPIC
FAMILY TRADITION AND HE'S DREAMED UP
AN UNFORGETTABLE PARTY!

ONLY, AFTER SEVERAL DISASTERS
INVOLVING A FLATTENED CHIHUAHUA
AND A CURSE FROM THE TOOTH FAIRY,
IT'S BEEN CANCELLED.

LOOK OUT FOR THIS
LAUGH-OUT-LOUD ADVENTURE FROM

JO SIMMONS

Jo Simmons began her working life as a journalist. She has written lots of brilliant, laugh-out-loud books for children, including the Pip Street Mysteries and the bestselling, award-winning *I Swapped My Brother on the Internet!*. Jo lives in Brighton with her husband, two boys and a scruffy, formerly Romanian street dog.

Nathan Reed has been illustrating
professionally since 2000. He has illustrated
other fiction series, including Grandma Dangerous
by Kita Mitchell and Sam Wu by Katie and Kevin
Tsang, as well as lots of picture books. Nathan
lives in London with his wife and two boys, and
when not illustrating, he can often be found
watching his beloved football team,
Tottenham Hotspur!

SUMMER HOLIDAYS? BORING!
TINY ISLAND? BORING!
A DODO – A WHAT?! YES!

THIS WILL
BE THE WILDEST
SUMMER EVER!

LOOK OUT FOR THIS
LAUGH-OUT-LOUD ADVENTURE FROM

JO SIMMONS

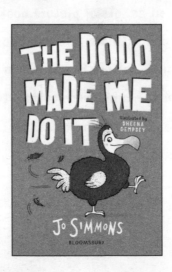